A Shot At Amore

Nora James

16pt

Read How You Want
LARGE PRINT BOOKS, BRAILLE & DAISY

Copyright Page from the Original Book

TABLE OF CONTENTS

A Shot at Amore
Nora James

Second chance love has never been so alluring ... or dangerous.

When Sofia returns to the small town of Sant'Agosto in Central Italy to take care of her sick aunt, she doesn't expect to find Antonio, her childhood sweetheart, there. He's back from Rome, has turned into the sexiest man alive—and he carries a gun. That's because, as Vice-Commander of a special operations group, he fights the Mafia on a daily basis.

Can Antonio be trusted with Sofia's heart? Or will he disappoint her as he did when they were teens?

For Antonio, the situation is even more fraught: should he push Sofia away to protect her from his dangerous world, or let her love him although it could cost her life?

About the author

Nora James grew up in Australia, before spending several years in Paris where she studied, worked and met the Frenchman who would soon become her husband. In her mid-twenties she returned to Western Australia with her spouse, read law at UWA and travelled extensively through her employment as an international resources lawyer and translator.

In 2016 she and her husband returned to France. She now writes novels from the home in coastal Brittany that the couple share with their daughter and a menagerie of furry friends.

When Nora's not dreaming up stories she can be found in the garden growing vegetables, in the kitchen cooking up a storm or on the couch reading a good book.

She loves interacting with readers. You can follow her and contact her through her Facebook page https://www.facebook.com/authornorajames or her website www.norajames.com.au.

Acknowledgements

To my gorgeous husband Dominique and my wonderful daughter Elise, thank you for your love and your belief in me. I couldn't do what I do without you. I couldn't do anything without you. Some days, I can't do anything with you, but it's a small price to pay for all the happiness.

To Nicola Robinson, a very big thank you for your guidance and support, and all the time you put into each project. I must have done something good in a previous life to find you.

To Brooke Halliwell, Johanna Baker and the entire team at Escape Publishing and HarperCollins, I'm grateful for everything you do, from the editing to the book covers and every other form of assistance and promotion. I'm the worst person in the world to do those things, so you are angels to me.

To Claire Boston, Anna Jacobs, Juanita Kees, Teena Raffa-Mulligan and Susanna Rogers of the Fine Print Critique Group, thanks for your invaluable advice and friendship. You're the smartest bunch of women on the west coast of Australia. Possibly on the west coast of every continent, come to think of it.

To my readers, you deserve the biggest thanks of all. You are the reason there are authors and books, and I know I can rely on your wonderful imagination to make my stories come to life.

To Pasquale A., judge Giovanni Falcone and all those who spend their lives fighting evil. You have my eternal admiration and gratitude. As does my grandmother, nonna Angela, although perhaps for different reasons.

1

Chapter 1

Death was a distinct possibility. Was that why Nella was sweating profusely, or was it the heat of the Italian summer? Sofia wiped the brow of the woman who'd been a mother to her with a cloth dampened in icy water and smiled, clinging to hope against all odds the way she always did.

'Better?' She carefully perched at the end of the chunky velvet couch, mindful not to sit on Nella's emaciated feet. Since the latest round of chemotherapy, the sofa was where the frail woman spent most of her time, lying in front of the television that she left on as a distraction but never watched.

'*Si*, much better, *cara mia*.' Nella tucked a strand of her sparse hair behind her ear, a pure white lock when before she contracted leukaemia it had been as thick and dark as Sofia's curls.

'You're not comfortable, are you, *zia?*'

'I'll be fine. You sit down.'

Sofia performed a little dance. 'These legs are itching to move around. Come on. How can I help? Just tell me and I'm yours.'

Nella giggled. 'You're an angel. Stupid old body, shivering one minute and too hot the next.

Do you think you could open that window over there for me?'

'Sure.' It would let in some air, although probably not cool. The choice was more often than not between hot and stinking hot in central Italy on a summer afternoon.

Nella sighed. 'I wish you didn't have to do all this for me.'

'It's nothing at all. What else do I have on my plate?' She had a whole year off teaching and no husband to worry about. Not since she'd managed to free herself from that control freak two years ago. 'Besides, you looked after me when I had no one, remember?'

Nella groaned with discomfort as she turned on her side, shifting the embroidered sheet that hid her legs. 'Your mother never should have let that rotten scoundrel talk his way into her pants. Your father wouldn't have lost the plot if she'd behaved the way a wife should.'

Sofia wasn't so sure. Her father, Nella's brother, had been mentally fragile for as long as she remembered, but it wasn't worth arguing about. 'Nothing can change the past, zia Nella. I, for one, make a point of never looking back.' She swung open the window panes hoping for a cool breeze to make its way down from the surrounding mountains and into the valley, rustling in the olive trees before whipping past the spicy-scented red geraniums and through the roughly rendered white house, but today the air was still. She sighed, about to sit back down, when a car pulled up in front of the country property. 'Someone's here. A black hatchback. A Lancia, I think.'

An impressive man stepped out of it, broad shouldered, dark-haired, an elegant silhouette that stood ramrod straight on the dusty dirt road in front of their ornate wrought iron gate. 'A very tall man. He's just standing there, talking on the phone. Shall I let him in?'

'*Dio mio.* What day is it today?'

'Tuesday.'

Nella covered her face with her hands. 'My memory's letting me down.'

'That's normal, *zia*. They told you that you might get chemo fog.'

'He phoned yesterday while you were watering the eggplant and tomatoes. I was so happy to hear he was coming over and then it went and slipped my mind. Quick, pass me that hairbrush, *bella mia*.'

Sofia smiled. She hadn't seen her aunt panic like that before. Was it a man Nella wanted to impress? Why else would she want to do her hair? 'Who is it, *zia*?'

'The General.'

Sofia's eyebrows shot up. A General? How did her simple, country aunt know such a high-ranking official?

'Is he on his own, Sofia? There was a rumour circulating about him getting divorced.'

'Well, it's just him today.'

'Hurry up, come closer and sit.' Nella grabbed the tarnished gold hairbrush off her as she approached.

Sofia let out a cry when she felt the bristles against her own scalp. 'Zia! What are you doing? I thought you wanted to tidy *your* hair, not *mine!*'

'There, you're beautiful.'

'I have to look good because you have a General friend with a row of medals on his jacket?'

'He isn't actually a General. But everybody's sure it will happen soon. Such a brilliant man. I bet he'll have all those medals before he's even forty. He's already an important man and if I remember correctly he's only two years older than you, so that means he's...'

'Thirty-seven. You don't remember how old I am, do you?'

'He's even on TV sometimes. Very high up in the *carabinieri*.'

'What does he do exactly?' asked Sofia as the bell rang. 'His job title, I mean.'

'Get the remote, *cara mia,* and let him in.'

Sofia found the button and pressed it, and the automatic gate opened with a clunk.

'Me and titles...' Nella shrugged. 'He's second in charge of some special unit in Rome. He fights the really bad criminals, the Mafia and the like.'

'That's impressive.' And dangerous, but why worry Nella by pointing that out about her friend?

'You hadn't heard that's what he'd become? He'll be happy to see *you* again.'

'Excuse me?' Happy to see *her*? *Again*? Sofia didn't know anyone on his way to being a General. Who was this man? Before she had a chance to ask, confident footsteps had reached their door.

'*Permesso?*' His voice was deep and mellow as he asked for permission to enter, the kind you longed to hear on a star-filled night.

'*Vieni*, my angel!' called Nella, as he stood in the doorway, his neck slightly bent to accommodate his tall frame. 'Come on in.'

The man entered and Sofia studied his face. There was something familiar about that square jaw of his. Familiar and very attractive.

He kissed Nella on both cheeks. 'I heard the news. I'm so sorry, Nella. How are you holding up?'

'I'm feeling weak but OK. It's fine, really, whatever happens. I've lived seventy-three wonderful years. And I'm still here. They said it could take a turn for the worst, but they're not always good at predicting things, and you know me. I don't give up that easily. I've been fighting this with everything I've got.'

'I'm glad you're in good spirits.'

She patted his back before turning to Sofia. 'You remember my niece, Sofia, I'm sure. She's put her teaching career on hold and come all the way from Australia to take care of her old *zia*.'

He glanced at Sofia sideways with his grey-green eyes and the electricity in them sent a jolt down her spine. But a certain darkness in his gaze told her that she wasn't a good memory for him. He grunted out a greeting. '*Buongiorno*.'

Nella waved her hands about. 'Oh, come on, you two. You're acting like you don't know each other.'

Sofia stared at her aunt and shrugged.

'It's Antonio. Surely you remember him. Before moving to Rome he and his family lived up in the mountains and sometimes spent holidays down here in the house next door to cousin Mario. He was here the two years you lived with us. Our little Nino. Of course he's changed a bit. We all have. That was over twenty years ago.'

Nino. The memory hit Sofia like a tornado, lifting her into the sky, spinning her around, stealing her breath until she thought she would suffocate. So much for never looking back.

Unbelievable. The teen who followed me everywhere on his Vespa that summer. He even crashed it once because he couldn't take his eyes off me instead of watching where he was going.

And it was the same for me.

She'd spent so many days, so many nights, dreaming of him, longing for his touch and a taste of his lips. She'd written his initials next to hers on the inside of her make-up case, and whispered his name before falling asleep. But then there'd been that evening on the balcony. He'd made her feel like she didn't matter, like she'd *never* mattered. Perhaps she'd overreacted after that. She'd regretted how she'd behaved, even if he'd deserved it.

Antonio De Santis. Oh, boy.

He was broader, much more muscular than before and time had chiselled his jaw, but when she studied his grey-green eyes a little longer she found the magnetic gaze of the seventeen-year-old she once knew. It really was him. How she'd wanted to press her lips against his all those years ago! Who'd have thought she'd ever bump into him again?

Now she was expected to kiss him politely on the cheeks, Italian style, by way of greeting. It would be terribly rude not to. She took a couple of steps towards him and leaned closer. His spiced citrus scent opened her lungs and made her want to take the deepest of breaths, as if she were about to plunge into the sparkling Mediterranean sea, diving into a deep and distant past, unable to resurface for so long that she was bound to lack oxygen. Instead, she hid her reaction as the light perfume mixed with the ever so enticing scent of his skin went to her head.

They kissed quickly in the most formal way, cheeks barely touching, but it was enough to awaken all of Sofia's senses, enough to make her shiver the way she once had when she was near Antonio. Did he remember the moment they'd shared behind the church? She'd been on her way to her cousin Oxana's house and had bumped into him as she'd cut through the jasmine-scented church gardens late that afternoon. She'd rested against the ancient stone wall, and he had leaned forward and gently removed an oleander petal from her hair. To the song of the cicadas, in over thirty degree heat, she'd shivered.

Oh, how she'd shivered!

'I had no idea you were here, Sofia, or...'
His deep, warm voice had an edge to it now.
Or what? He wouldn't have come?

Nella waved her arms about. 'Bring those
two chairs over here, Sofia love, so you can both
sit down next to me.'

Sofia carried a carved ladder back chair to
the couch.

'Would you mind fetching that bottle of
apricot juice and some glasses, please? Some
biscotti, too, *bella mia*. You'll have juice, right,
Nino? Or coffee?'

'Coffee with two sugars. If it's no trouble.'

Sofia forced a smile. 'No trouble at all.' It
would get her out of the living room and away
from him for a few minutes and she desperately
needed that.

She entered the kitchen, breathing in the
vague but comforting smell of spaghetti and
thyme, and rested her back against the cupboards
for an instant to give her heart, that was beating
fast enough to fuel a rocket into space, a chance
to slow down. She made an espresso, the scent
of the ground beans now filling the air, poured
a glass of apricot juice for Nella, placed the star
aniseed biscuits onto a fancy plate and lay
everything out on a silver tray.

*One more minute. I just have to get through
one minute and I'm out of here.*

She returned to the living room and slid the tray onto the small table next to Nella.

'Here you are: coffee, apricot juice and biscotti. I have to pick up a few things in town.' She grabbed her handbag and her keys. 'So I'll leave you two in peace.'

Nella's eyes rounded with surprise. 'Sorry? What do you need so badly that you have to go right now? And the car's being fixed, remember? Paolo won't bring it back until tomorrow or the end of the week if he hasn't got the right part.'

Sofia couldn't help but chuckle at the exaggerated outrage on her aunt's face. 'I'll walk, zia. It's not that far.'

'Antonio can take you into town,' suggested Nella quickly. 'He'll be heading back that way. Isn't that so, Antonio? Or are you going straight back to Rome?'

'I'll be staying in town for a while.'

'A holiday?'

'Of sorts.'

Nella grinned. 'Bravo! That's good to hear. How long are you here for?'

'I don't know exactly. Maybe a month.'

'You'll come and see me, then?'

'I certainly will.'

'Often?'

'As often as you want.'

'Every day, in that case?'

He let out a surprised laugh.

Sofia took a deep breath. 'Every day is a lot to ask of anyone. I'm here for everything you need, *zia*.' She certainly didn't want to see Antonio De Santis every day. Not anymore. Not like when she used to sit in the garden, picking at grapes under the patio, in the hope that he'd ride by on his Vespa, her heart beating faster every time the sound of an engine resonated through the peaceful countryside. Seeing him every day had been her greatest desire then.

'I know you're here, Sofia, and I really appreciate it, but a few minutes with someone else would be nice. For you, too, *cara*. It can't be healthy for you to be with nobody but me. And I haven't caught up with Antonio for such a long time. It'll be like back in the old days when you and your family visited all summer, hey, Nino *mio*.'

The General cleared his throat. 'I should be able to fit that in.'

'*Grazie*,' said Nella, beaming. 'You can call in any time that suits you, day or night. After all, I'm always here.' She chuckled. 'Seriously, I don't sleep like I used to. I catch half an hour here and there, so even pop in late if you want to. You'll definitely come?'

'Sure. You can count on it.'

'How nice! Something to look forward to every day! So, do you want to take Sofia to the shops now?'

'Well, um...' He let out his breath. 'I wasn't planning on leaving straight away. I thought we'd have a chat, Nella, but I suppose if you want me to drive Sofia, you and I can catch up tomorrow.' He threw Sofia an uneasy glance.

Sofia held up her hand. 'No, you stay right there. I insist. The walk will do me good.' She could tell he wasn't keen to give her a lift, and she could imagine how uncomfortable she would feel next to him in the car. She smiled politely as she donned a straw hat.

Nella lifted her gaze to the ceiling. 'There's no need to run away. *Mamma mia*. Look at this niece of mine behaving like an embarrassed teenager!'

Before the well-intentioned older woman could inadvertently add anything more humiliating, Sofia slipped out the door, hurried up the driveway to the gate and escaped, heading to Sant'Agosto as fast as she could, even if there was nothing pressing on her shopping list and, on a day like today, when it was neither market day nor a 'festa', a religious celebration when every street came alive with music, laughter, and stalls laden with small knick-knacks, treats and cheap souvenirs, there was little to do in the sleepy country town nestled in the valley about halfway between Rome and Naples.

That didn't matter to Sofia. The only thing she desperately needed in town right now was to get away from Nino.

***

Antonio sat in the driver's seat, unsure of what had shaken him more: the sight of kind Nella, white-haired, thin, and completely helpless on the couch, or having to stand so close to Sofia again. Having to smell Sofia's scent without being able to touch her, having to talk to her without saying what was in his heart. Still. After all these years.

He whispered her name, *Sofia Conti.*

To have to come here every single day! Why on earth had he agreed to that?

Because Nella has cancer and at her age the prognosis isn't good. How do you say 'no' to the dying?

He closed his car door and tooted the horn gently before driving off, another goodbye to the woman who had been such a good friend to his family, in case she ... He took a deep breath. Well, just in case.

If his own parents had been able to, they would have come to visit Nella, would have shown her all the love and respect they had for her. But they had left the country, acquired new identities and been in hiding since the 'accident' that nearly killed them. They were tucked away in an overseas place Antonio didn't even dare think about, as if the Mafia could get into his head and find his mother and father in the corners of his imagination.

And now he too had been forced into disappearing for a while, keeping a low profile when he'd had enough of hiding—but his boss had ordered him away, applying work policies to the letter. At least Antonio was in his own car, not an imposing bullet-proof, bomb-proof State vehicle with the latest safety gizmos, which he'd flat out refused to drive and thankfully wasn't mentioned in the internal document that ruled his life. While an armoured car would have offered protection, it was hardly ever enough to stop the Mafia. Look at Judge Falcone. His armoured four-wheel drive had been blown to smithereens, and half the freeway with it. Besides, was there anything more *noticeable* than a big imposing vehicle? Sometimes Antonio wondered about the thinking behind all these office policies.

He took the last bend before town, passing the house with the distinctive balcony and its succession of columns that he always glanced at whenever he drove by. He shook his head. That damn balcony! The memories ... His only hope was that they'd demolish the horrid *palazzo* one day to build something else in its place, something that wouldn't make him bite the inside of his lip every time he went by.

A few instants later he reached the paved town square, the heart of Sant'Agosto marked on one side by a stately fountain in front of the white shire building, on the other by the thirteenth-century stone church flanked by cypress trees where people gathered to exchange town gossip on balmy summer evenings. Between the two points, a handful of soft-pink and beige rendered shops and a couple of bars with terracotta roofs, their round tables spilling onto the footpath like waterlilies on a pond, provided the necessities of life and daily entertainment for the Sant'Agostians.

Antonio parked closest to the small cluster of shops and climbed out, relieved he hadn't come across Sofia on her way back home while he was driving into town. It was a good thing he hadn't had to give her a lift, a very good thing that she'd made her own way into Sant'Agosto. He didn't know how he'd have managed beside her in the car.

He needed something to steady his nerves and ease the knots in his shoulders. He entered the bar that faced the church, the one with the burgundy awnings above its windows, and the scent of coffee mixed with Strega liqueur filled his lungs. It was here that Antonio used to sit outside with his parents on a warm summer evening and eat gelato while watching the comings and goings of the whole town and the memory brought a smile to his face. Ice-cream wasn't what he had in mind today, though.

'*Buongiorno*. A glass of Chianti, please.' Normally he would have called the person behind the bar by their first name, would have known exactly who it was. 'Actually, make that a Campari.'

Today, he didn't recognise the adolescent who poured the alcohol, but he was certain the kid was related to someone whose roots were firmly anchored in this valley. No one new ever came to Sant'Agosto and everyone would be on their guard if a true outsider suddenly turned up. That's what made it safe for Antonio here. Relatively speaking. And it wasn't the village his family came from, only the place where they used to spend their summers when he was a teenager, so the hope was that it had gone unnoticed by the Mafia. It certainly wouldn't be the very first place they looked for him.

In any event it was much safer here for Antonio than Rome at the moment and a lot easier than being banished to some lost foreign country thousands of kilometres away or even a forgotten Italian village where he knew no one and had no idea who he could trust. If it had been entirely up to him, if he hadn't had orders to follow, Antonio would have stayed at work as if nothing had happened.

He didn't fear for his life. Not like he feared for the lives of those around him.

The young barman placed a small dish of olives next to his drink. 'Enjoying being in town?'

'Sure. I'm Antonio De Santis. My family holidayed here from time to time, the house on the other side of the church.' The home that belonged to a friend of his mother's, someone the Mafia wouldn't track down quite as easily or as fast as a relative. And if they did, so be it. He'd be waiting for them. He'd already had to ship his parents out of the country and have everyone believe they were dead. He'd had enough. He wasn't going to let the Mafia manipulate him into changing his life anymore.

A smile lit up the young barman's face. 'Yes, I know who you are, *signore*. My *mamma* mentioned you were in town.'

'Your mother?'

'Marina Banna.'

'You're *Marina's* son! Wow, you've grown!' The boy had certainly changed a lot. 'The last time I bumped into you, you must have been half your size. You're working now?'

'Just helping out over summer. Our family has the greatest respect for what you do for Italy, sir.'

I only do what's necessary. 'Thank you. It's nice of you to say. Give your parents my regards.'

Suddenly laughter floated through the air, a laugh Antonio would have recognised anywhere. A sound that had haunted his dreams for years, at times playful and seductive, at others cruel and cold. He closed his eyes. Of all the places in town, she had to be here, in this bar, at the same time as him.

Hopefully, Sofia hadn't seen him. He drank, guzzling down the entire contents of the glass of bittersweet ruby red *aperitivo*, and left the price of the drink and a few more Euros on the bar, before making his way to the main door, head down, sure he'd be able to slip through it unnoticed. And that's exactly where he found Sofia as the brass church bells marked noon, impossible to ignore as they clanged nearby. She was standing right in front of the glass entrance with another brunette in her early thirties and an older woman. There was no avoiding her now, and no escaping a polite exchange or else he and Sofia would be the talk of the town. Not that he cared, but she might.

She took a sharp breath when her gaze settled on him. 'Antonio.'

He nodded dutifully to acknowledge her in front of anyone who was, discreetly or not so discreetly, watching. 'Sofia. I left your aunt's side about twenty minutes ago. Maybe you should be heading home.'

He could have kicked himself. Like a teenager, he'd said the first thing that had sprung to mind, the absolutely stupid first thing, as if he'd learned nothing over the past twenty years. Bossing her around in front of everyone in town could only hinder their relationship.

His lip twisted.

Relationship? Do we have any such thing? Did we ever?

Sofia clicked her tongue with disapproval. 'I know how long I can leave Nella on her own, and she has my number.' She pulled her mobile phone out of her pocket and held it up. 'I'm contactable at all times and I don't need any *big shot* to tell me what to do or how to keep my aunt comfortable. But thank you, Nino, for your concern.'

'Right.' He swallowed his pride and walked by her, looking straight ahead. Regardless of how hard he'd worked to become who he was, it was clear that he wasn't a big shot in her eyes.

And hers were the only eyes that had mattered to him when he'd started this career. She was the only one who'd meant anything for so long. Years.

Everything he'd done, everything he'd sacrificed to prove his worth, had made no difference. He was still the young boy she'd thrown away like a dirty rag.

He steeled himself and made his way past the outside tables, the large round fountain of the *piazza* and up the cobblestone road, conscious of each step he took. When he reached the car, he curled his fingers around the handle of the vehicle's door and froze.

Just get in. Don't look at her. Don't look back.

The need to see her, to catch a glimpse of her dark curls, for their eyes to meet once more, was stronger than anything. Had she watched him walk away? Did she regret what she'd said to him, the way he'd immediately regretted his own words?

He turned around and glanced in her direction, his heart beating stronger than ever, before it suddenly sank.

Sofia wasn't looking at him with longing in her eyes.

She wasn't looking at him at all.

She was gone.

He let out a moan. He'd thought coming to the town where he'd spent his holidays as a kid would be better than running to an unknown place, thought it would be straightforward. That was before he knew Sofia was here.

It was patently clear to him now that his stay in Sant'Agosto was going to be anything but easy.

Chapter 2

Sofia finished sweeping the aged marble floor that had lost its shine and fluffed up the tapestry cushions in the living room. She glanced at the carved wooden clock that graced the wall above the velvet couch. Twenty past ten. Would Antonio come in the morning or the afternoon?

'It would have been so much easier if you'd agreed on a specific time with your General. It's a pain not knowing when he's going to turn up.' Like having a noose around your neck and no idea of when it would tighten.

Nella shrugged. 'He won't mind if there's something out of place when he visits. We live here. It isn't a museum. Well, if you can call this living.' She pointed to her skeletal body.

Before Sofia could answer, the bell chimed. *He's here.*

As she pressed the button on the remote control and opened the gate, a tingle of anticipation danced around her core. Why? She didn't particularly want to see Antonio. There'd been days long ago when she'd written every detail in her diary about him: how he'd worn a tight navy and white striped shirt with dark blue pants that showed off his flat stomach and muscular legs, that she'd caught a glimpse of him in town at 2.34pm precisely and hadn't taken another breath until 2.35pm. More often than not, she'd written about the way she'd trembled when her gaze had met his, like a butterfly fluttering its wings, and she'd been a little ashamed to be wallowing in Antonio's attention behind her aunt's back, but rather proud of it too. That's what you did when you were a teenager. You stole forbidden moments, built a fantasy and put it all in writing.

Now, she was a full-grown woman with her feet on the ground. No more irrational dreams, no more words written hastily while her aunt was in the bathroom or busy preparing lasagna for dinner, so as not to be discovered. Antonio was part of the past, nothing more, and Sofia wanted to keep it that way. She wrapped her arms around her belly. She wasn't kidding herself about him, was she? No, definitely not.

I don't need a man to tell me what to do, like he tried to at the bar in town.

A man to give her the cold shoulder if she came home ten minutes late. To check every payment, every cash withdrawal she made. And yell at her if she so much as glanced in the most innocent way in the direction of another guy. Walk around with blinkers on, that's what she'd had to do when she was married to Terry.

It had taken her a long time to free herself from his tyranny. She would never submit to that kind of miserable existence again. Not that she'd ever really *submitted* to it. It had crept up on her, infiltrated her, woven its evil tentacles around every fibre of her being slowly, imperceptibly, until she'd woken one day and realised that she had become a prisoner.

'*Permesso.*' Antonio knocked at the same time as his deep voice asked for permission to enter.

Nella's face lit up. '*Vieni,* Antonio.'

His light citrus scent filled the air and Sofia's heart beat faster as he leaned close and greeted her with a peck on each cheek. Thankfully he quickly moved over to her aunt and Sofia turned away to hide the heat rising in her. Stupid body. Why couldn't she control her physical reactions better?

'How are you today, Nella? May I?' He gestured to the chair next to the couch.

'Make yourself at home. You don't have to ask, Antonio. Sofia, would you get us some coffee, eh?'

'Sure, *zia.*'

'Bring some of those soft *amaretti* too. I love those biscuits. Let's see if my taste has returned.'

'No problem.' Sofia hurried into the kitchen, trying to ignore the way her nerves jumped around her belly. She prepared two cups of coffee, one decaffeinated for her aunt, and placed the little Italian biscuits made from almonds into a dish.

When she returned to the living area, Nella was interrogating Antonio. 'So how's Rosalba?'

'She's fine. At least, I think she is.'

'You *think?*' Nella raised an eyebrow.

'I ... uh, Rosalba and I aren't together anymore. We're actually recently divorced.'

'I'm sorry,' said Nella, smiling too noticeably at Sofia.

Embarrassment coloured Antonio's cheeks.

Poor man. That was hard for him to admit. I know the feeling. Too many people think divorce is failure when it can be just the opposite.

Sofia handed Antonio his coffee. 'Some biscuits too?'

He took a couple, nodding his thanks. She had planned on leaving straight away but she hadn't expected to feel sorry for the man. Should she stay a while? She hesitated until she thought of her own messed-up marriage. People who didn't know the whole story had probably pitied her ex-husband, too, and yet she'd been the victim.

Victim ... Horrible word. I was someone caught in a web for a while. Someone who's free now.

Perhaps Antonio had kept Rosalba under his thumb too. Perhaps he deserved to be alone.

Sofia reminded herself of what had happened in town, how he'd bossed her around. And then the way he'd treated her in the end when he was a teenager ... Maybe he hadn't changed much.

She took off the flip-flops she wore inside and slipped on her walking sandals.

Nella leaned forward. 'What are you doing, Sofia?'

'Getting a little exercise before it's too hot.'

'But it's already hot. You should go before eight in the morning or late in the afternoon. And Antonio's come over. Stay here with us, now.'

Antonio gazed at her with the magnetic eyes she remembered from her teens, those grey-green eyes she used to feel she might drown in, so much so she'd mentioned them to her cousin Oxana when she'd visited. The two girls had sat in the shade of the fig tree, all the way down the back of the sprawling rural property where no one could eavesdrop, and had spent the afternoon giggling and talking about boys. That is, Oxana had told her about quite a few boys, while Sofia had only mentioned Antonio and his mesmerising gaze because for her, there'd been no one else. *It sounds like you're in love,* Oxana had said and Sofia had simply gasped, not knowing what to answer.

Those days were long gone. Perhaps things would have turned out differently if he hadn't made her feel so worthless that night on the balcony, but whatever they'd shared was well and truly over now.

It was over, wasn't it?

So why was it she could barely breathe in Antonio's presence? Why was her whole body on alert? With a huff, she dismissed the feeling, annoyed with herself. It was nothing but a superficial response to his charms, merely physical, nothing to do with the heart or the mind. Physical attraction was a curse, a chemical reaction of no value. It drew you to all the wrong people, trapped you there like a wild animal in a cage. Who needed it? Not her.

'Earth to Sofia, hello?' Nella waved in her direction, jolting Sofia out of her thoughts.

'Sorry. I, hmm, I was somewhere else.'

'We can see that, Sofia.'

As heat rose in her cheeks, she pretended to pick fluff off her top. 'I was just thinking, Antonio, you know how you've agreed to come over every day to see *zia* Nella?'

His eyebrows shot up and his neck moved forward as he listened attentively to her.

'Well, how about you come here at the same time every day? That way I can get into the habit of exercising while you are here.' She placed her hands on her hips and looked him in the eye. 'It would be better for Nella, so she's not left too long on her own. As you mentioned when we bumped into each other in town, it's best if someone is with her *at all times.*' His unpleasant remark, that Nella had been on her own long enough, had come in handy now, a perfectly good reason for Sofia to escape every time he visited.

He let out a sound in between a chuckle and a gasp. 'I didn't mean it like that.'

Nella, puzzled, looked from one to the other. 'What comment? What happened?'

'Nothing, *zia*. Don't worry about it.'

'I'll see what I can do,' said Antonio with a frown. 'I might not be able to come over at exactly the same time every day, because of work. From time to time I have to attend to urgent matters.'

His phone rang and he held up a finger as he answered, stepping purposefully into the corridor. Exchanging a glance, the women listened, Sofia perching at the end of the couch. 'Yes. Yes. No. Yes. Tonight? OK.'

He hung up without a goodbye and returned to the lounge room, his expression a closed book.

'Everything all right?' Nella pushed herself up on her elbows with a groan.

He nodded. 'Fine. It's just the office.'

Sofia dropped her gaze to the floor. What did work want with him *tonight*?

'I thought you were on holidays,' said Nella.

'Of sorts. I have to follow things up even when I'm away. When you're in a job like mine you can never really switch off.'

'What exactly do you do, Antonio?' asked Sofia, curious. '*Zia* Nella wasn't sure of your job title.'

'I'm the Vice-Commander of the ROS, the—'

'The *raggruppamento operativo speciale*?' interrupted Sofia. Like everyone in Italy and interested people abroad too, she'd heard about the special unit of the *carabinieri* that fought organised crime. It was mentioned in the papers and on TV often enough.

'Yes. I used to be in charge of the unit that fought the *Ndrangheta*, the Mafia down south in Calabria, but now I'm taking care of Rome.'

'You'd have your work cut out for you,' said Sofia.

'For sure. It never stops. That's why it's hard for me to commit to being here every day at the same time. I sometimes have to do urgent work on the computer, get people organised and so on. There's a lot of pressure in the job. But you'd be under pressure in a classroom, too, I imagine, Sofia. Kids these days are notoriously difficult.'

Sofia chuckled. 'Sure, although I expect working in a school isn't quite as dangerous as what you do.'

Nella threw one hand up in the air. 'I have an idea! Why don't you come here at ten every morning and bring your computer with you, Antonio? That way, you can stay without a worry, for as long as you like. You could have lunch with us every day. And if you have your work things with you and something urgent crops up you can always attend to it straight away. You'd be comfortable in the study. No one would disturb you in there. I'd quite like to hear you typing away, actually. We could do with a bit more life in the house. Sofia can go off on her walk for an hour and then when she comes back she can make lunch for all of us. What's one more person at the table? It's virtually the same whether you're preparing for two or for three. Sofia is an excellent cook. *Spaghetti alle vongole, panzanella, risotto,* you name it, she can make it for you.'

Sofia clicked her tongue to attract her aunt's attention and stared at her with rounded eyes. What on earth was Nella thinking? It was bad enough to want him to hang around every day for an hour or so. But inviting him to stay half the day, every day? That was completely crazy. Why didn't she ask him to move in, while she was at it?

Nella sought her niece's gaze. 'Good idea, hey, Sofia?'

'Why don't we play it by ear? I wouldn't want to impose on Antonio.' She glanced at him, quite certain he'd agree, although she couldn't read his expression. 'And I don't think we have much in the fridge right now.'

Antonio raised both hands. 'Don't worry, I have other plans for today.'

Sofia jumped to her feet, placed her phone and a small bottle of water in a pouch that she tossed over her shoulder, pulled her straw hat over her ears and nodded to their guest. 'I'll be off, then.'

'Really?' asked Nella, disappointment in her eyes.

Sofia smiled sincerely at her aunt, and politely at their guest, before walking stiffly to the door, conscious of the General's gaze on her. 'I'll see you later, Antonio.'

Or not. With a bit of luck you'll be gone when I come home.

That was how she liked it. Just Nella and her, the house to themselves. They didn't need anyone else. A man hanging around spelt nothing but trouble.

A man named Antonio spelt total disaster.

Chapter 3

Sofia stepped into the garden and took a deep breath, oxygen finally filling her lungs properly for the first time since Antonio had turned up today.

At the end of the large country block, the clunk of the metal gate of the fully enclosed property relaxed her shoulders as it shut behind her. She was truly away now, off on her own on the peaceful dirt road. Lizards scattered as her feet brushed against the grass that lined the country lane. Birds flew overhead, the whoosh of their wings so close at times that she could nearly catch them with her bare hands.

She walked by a farm where an old woman dressed in black from head to toe sat on a bench, watching her intently, and by another where a man was leading a donkey towards the back of the house.

She passed field after field of freshly laboured land waiting to be planted with crops, others shaded with olive trees, the perfect place for a picnic with a friend.

With a man.

With someone like ... Antonio.

Antonio? What the hell am I thinking?

Why did the thought burrow its way into her mind? And why the memories that came flooding back during her walk as if a dam had broken? Like the time Antonio had walked up the hill next to her in complete silence behind the procession of Santa Maria del Carmine. Sofia had barely spent a second admiring the gold-laden painted statue of the saint, the pretty town illuminated for the occasion, or the fireflies that sparkled as they flitted about in the dark as if to announce the magic to come. She'd seen nothing but Nino, around every bend and up the narrow lanes, all the way to the highest point of the town, and her stomach had turned inside out every time he'd looked her way.

It was long ago, so long ago.

As her feet pounded the dry road, Sofia took a deep breath and forced herself to empty her mind. She directed her gaze to the mountains in the distance and the way their outline blurred with the bright sky, as if a painter had softened their edge with his brush.

A moment later, she found herself grinning to herself once again. It was a day as luminous as today that she'd waited in line at the *gelateria* near the bridge in Sant'Agosto, and Nino had come out with two cups of ice-cream. He'd held out one for her, pear and pistachio, winking at her before taking off. She hadn't even known that he'd been in the shop, whereas he'd spotted her there in the queue on the footpath and decided to buy her the gelato. But how had he known her favourite flavours?

She shook herself. Just because she'd dreamed of him as a teen didn't mean he was anything to her now. Just because they'd shared a few moments, moments that at the end of the day had amounted to nothing, wasn't a reason for her to go down that road again. She'd do well to remember how Antonio had made her feel that night on the balcony. The conclusion of their fling, if you could call it that, had been more than disappointing. It had brought her pain she didn't want to recall. If only he'd made the effort to get to know her beforehand. If only he'd cared enough to take the time. She, too, had dreamed of kissing him, of holding him, of more, much more.

Just not like that. Not the way things had happened that night. He'd made her feel like she was nothing as a young girl. He'd broken her heart at such a tender age.

What was the point of reminiscing? She sighed and concentrated once more on the glorious nature around her, the bees buzzing in the wildflowers, the silky sheet of pure blue sky.

Soon, a tinny engine broke the calm of the morning. An old faded red Fiat was heading her way, a cloud of dust billowing behind it. Sofia shifted to the side as much as she could, but the driver made no effort to steer clear of her. She jumped back out of caution and a sense of self-preservation, no longer used to these tiny Italian lanes after the wide streets of Australia. As she landed on the uneven ground on the side of the road, she twisted her ankle in a deep ditch hidden under the long grass and went tumbling down into the field.

Once she'd gathered her bearings a little, she rubbed her ankle to lessen the pain, letting out a cry. She stopped touching it, and purposefully slowed her breathing.

When she tried to stand, she screamed again. It hurt more than a slap, more than a shove. And she'd had a few of those.

She waited.

It's the shock, that's all. I'll be good to go in a few more minutes.

After resting for a while Sofia tried again, but she still couldn't put her foot down properly without groaning. She could put it down a little, though. That was a good sign, wasn't it? She managed to hobble closer to the side of the road but there was no way she'd be able to quickly get over the deep hole that had been dug alongside it as far as the eye could see, probably for water drainage of the field she'd landed in. Or as a fire break. Whatever the reason, it was most inconvenient to her.

She rubbed her forehead. She had to call home.

She dialled the number. 'It's me, *zia*.'

'I thought you'd be back by now. Is everything all right?'

'Yes, fine. I just walked a lot further than I realised. It's going to take me quite a while to get back.' Especially hopping on one leg. And before that, she had to figure out a way to climb back onto the road.

'But it's nearly lunch time! I'm already hungry, Sofia.'

'I'm sorry. I know you like to eat on time.'

'And so do you. Are you sure everything is all right? You sound a little rattled.' Her aunt knew her too well.

'Absolutely. All fine.'

'Hang on a minute, *cara*, will you?' Nella mumbled something Sofia couldn't make out, probably talking to herself as she often did, before adding, 'Where are you exactly?'

'On via Oliveto. A few minutes after the turnoff to Portarossa.'

'Via Oliveto, just after the road to Portarossa,' Nella repeated. 'You did walk quite a long way, didn't you?'

'Yes. It was so peaceful out here.' She'd definitely needed the peace, definitely needed to calm her nerves because ... Because of Antonio, and yet she'd gone and spent most of her time thinking about him on her walk.

'You're just like your old aunty. I used to love my summer strolls. Sometimes I went all the way up to Cerrano, to the old chapel, the tiny white one built into the hill.'

'I know. I remember. You were still doing that when I was a teen.'

'I loved seeing the little pink cyclamens hiding under the shrubs in spring, the fields of red poppies a bit later. Passing the houses and smelling the baking, the mix of lemon and aniseed. Taking a peek through gates to see if people had repainted their shutters or planted more pots. You see so much more on foot than when you zoom by in a car. Those were the days. Enjoy your youth, Sofia. Too many of us take it for granted, when it's such a blessing to be fit and healthy like you are now.'

Sofia stared at her ankle. 'Yep. As fit as an athlete.'

'Well, you stop right there, sweetheart. Antonio is on his way to get you. It won't take him long in the car.'

'What? He's still there?'

'He's been waiting for you to come home.'

A sense of panic grew in Sofia, working its way through her stomach like a worm through an apple. 'There's no need for him to go out of his way like that. I'll be back soon. Tell him I'm fine.' She paused but her aunt remained silent. 'Zia, would you please tell him he doesn't have to come for me? I don't need help.'

'It's too late, sweetheart. He was gone the minute he heard the name of the street.'

***

Antonio passed the road to Portarossa and scoured the horizon as far as he could see, taking in the small farms on either side, their rows of olive trees, their large chook pens, their vegetable patches big enough to feed an army, but there was no sign of Sofia. His jaw tightened. Had something bad happened to her?

He shook himself. He was doing it again, always thinking of the worst when he hadn't even reached the road junction that Sofia had indicated. In any case, there were no known ties between Sofia and him, and the Mafia wasn't looking for him here in Sant'Agosto, at least not that he knew. He had to stop thinking like when he was at work, always on full alert, and learn to take a breather. How did you do that when fighting organised crime had shaped your entire life?

As he approached the point where Sofia had said she was, he slowed right down, the car crawling up the dirt road in a cloud of dust. Suddenly something moved in the field. Was that a flash of colour down there? He did a double take. Her yellow top! He quickly pulled over and jumped out of the car. 'Sofia?'

'Over here.' She waved her hand about.

Something was wrong. She wasn't on her feet.

'Sofia!' He ran to her, his heart in his throat. He found her on the ground, one leg bent, the other stretched out, propped up on her elbows in the shade of a tree. Conscious. Check. No blood. Check. No gun pointed at her head. Check. Nothing nearby where men could hide, ready to shoot. Check. 'Are you all right? What happened?'

She shrugged. 'Nothing much. It's stupid really, I twisted my ankle, that's all.'

He let out his breath, relief washing over him.

'Here? In a field?'

'No. I was on the road. I jumped back when a car came by too fast, and fell because of the stupid ditch over there. I crawled over here into the shade when *zia* Nella said you were coming for me. You didn't have to come and get me, Antonio. I could have made it home on my own.

I'm a very good hopper, a champion Hopscotcher as a matter of fact.'

He laughed. He didn't know if she really was a champion Hopscotcher, but she was quite a character, there was no doubt about that. 'I'm sure you are, although Nella would appreciate you getting back before midnight.'

He took her hand in his and pulled her to her feet. Her small, soft hand that fit perfectly in his like it always had. He wanted to hold onto it for hours.

'Thanks.' She looked away. 'I'll be OK now. I might need a bit of help getting over the ditch.' She nodded to encourage him and he reluctantly let go of her. She hopped once, holding out her arms for balance.

He didn't dare insist that she put her weight on him. She was the most stubborn woman he'd ever known. No, not stubborn, wilful.

Strong. Independent. Proud. I like that about her.

He walked closer to her, his arm on his hip so it would be easy for her to grab him if she needed to. If she wanted to.

She hopped once more, wobbling, then gently placed her fingers on his forearm.

'I'm sorry,' she whispered.

'Don't be.' There was no reason whatsoever for her to be sorry. Being next to her, her light touch against his arm, was enough to make him vibrate. He definitely wasn't sorry about that.

She glanced at him. 'You have better things to do than take care of old ladies and rescue injured princesses.'

'Now then, I wouldn't refer to you as an old lady. Not quite.' He held back a smile, waiting for her reaction like a dog waits for a treat.

She huffed with exaggerated disgust and let go of him long enough to slap him playfully on the upper arm. 'You'll pay for that.'

'Why am I not surprised?' He grinned and when she smiled back, her eyes twinkling with glee, his stomach performed a triple somersault. Did she have to be so beautiful?

She leaned on him again, a little more this time, and the desire to pull her close, to feel her skin against his, grew in him.

They arrived at the ditch that separated them from the road. 'I'll carry you over,' he ventured. *Please God, make her accept. I want to hold her one more time.*

'No, that's not necessary. I just need to hang onto your arm.'

His heart sank. He opened his mouth to tell her that she wouldn't manage, but closed it again. If she'd decided to do it that way, none of his objections would change her mind.

Holding onto his arm, she hopped and screamed as she slipped. He pulled her back just in time to stop her from landing in the ditch. 'All right, that's enough.' He didn't care how much she objected or how strongly she wanted to prove that she was independent and self-sufficient, he wasn't going to stand by and watch her injure herself again.

He scooped her up and carried her in his arms.

'Put me down!' She wriggled about like a worm.

'The ground is too uneven. You'll end up twisting your other ankle, or breaking your neck, and then what? Just relax. I'm only carrying you back to the car.'

She stayed still and he held her a little closer. How he'd wanted to carry her like this that evening on the balcony! How he'd dreamed of leaving with her in his arms, snuggled up against his body! Instead, he'd gone home on his own without a word. It had been the loneliest night of his life.

He breathed in, her perfume filling his lungs. If he stopped, if he closed his eyes and rested his head against hers, he'd be back on that balcony with her, only this time she'd say yes. And then he'd be in Heaven.

Because Heaven is where Sofia is.

He reached the car, wishing he'd parked further away, and placed Sofia gently on the ground, his gaze meeting hers while she stood against him. What if he slowly bent his neck towards her, closer, closer again, until their lips touched? If he kissed her now, what would she do?

He groaned, annoyed with himself, and took a step back. He'd do well to remember her parting words that fateful night. *I'm not yours. I'll never be.*

She'd made it crystal clear how she felt back then. Was it still the case? Had she changed her mind since her teens? Was he game enough to find out?

He opened the car door. 'Do you need a hand climbing in?'

'No, it's OK, thanks.' She was breathless, when he was the one who'd done all the walking and the carrying. Was it being in his arms, and standing so close to him, that had robbed her of her oxygen? Had it affected her the way it had him? Her chest rising as she took a deep breath, she slid into the passenger seat.

He crouched down beside her. 'Let me take a look at it. I've seen a lot of injuries in my job.' He gently took her ankle in his hand and examined it, trying his best not to think of any other part of Sofia's body, of anything but Sofia's health. He pressed it slowly around the tendons, asked her if she could move it without pain when she didn't put her weight on it.

'I'm reasonably confident it isn't broken,' he said once he'd finished, cautiously placing her foot down on the mat. 'But I'm not a doctor. You ought to get a professional to check it, to be sure. And keep it elevated in the meantime.'

He walked to the driver's side, performed a three-point turn on the narrow dirt road and drove back towards Nella's house.

'Don't worry about me, Antonio, I'll be fine,' she said as the terracotta roof and white walls of the simple but pleasing double-storey building, with its wooden windows and washed green shutters, appeared around the bend. 'You can leave me at the gate. I'll hop down to the house. No uneven ground here.'

'What on earth are you talking about? You're injured, Sofia. It'll take me two seconds to carry you inside. Or at least let me offer you my arm to walk you down there.'

'I appreciate it, Antonio, I do, but it's not necessary. It's just a little sprain.' She crossed her arms and edged away from him.

'As you wish.' He held back a sigh. His whole being told him to protect her and she wouldn't let him. 'You're sure you don't need any help inside? Or dropping off at the doctor's?'

'No, thank you. I'm not going to let a little soreness to the ankle get in the way of anything. I have one good leg and on flat ground I should be able to either put the heel of my injured foot down, or use the tip of my toes. The doctor does house visits early morning, anyway. I'll make an appointment for tomorrow and he can come over. I think he starts at ten.'

'Good. In that case, I'll be around to hear what he has to say, since that's when I'm supposed to be calling in so you can exercise.' Although he was quite sure she wouldn't be exercising for a while.

'Fabulous. I'm looking forward to going out for a walk every morning at that time. I mean, maybe not tomorrow but soon. As soon as this stupid ankle is better.'

'And I'll stay a little once you get back, perhaps have a coffee, and go home. I do have things to do. I'm sure Nella will understand.' And he didn't want to impose on them for lunch every day, especially since Sofia seemed somewhat reluctant about that.

'We have a deal. A coffee after my walk sounds great.'

He quickly took in her expression. Did she really think it great to see him every day, even if only for a coffee? Her gaze shifted from him to the front window and then to the side window.

She's undecided. He smiled. Undecided was better than not wanting him around at all.

He cleared his throat. 'That said, while the plan is that I come over for a short while every morning, I actually think I should stay with you all day for the next couple of days and give the two of you a hand until you're back on your feet. I can do your errands and little jobs, if you like, since you're injured.'

'That's so kind of you,' said Sofia, her expression serious. 'But honestly you don't have to. Nella and I will be fine, just the two of us.'

He parked and climbed out of the car.

'What are you doing, Antonio? You don't need to get out. You were just dropping me off, that's all.'

'If you don't want my help to get you to the house, that's okay with me. I'm still going to stick my head through the doorway and let Nella know what's happening.' He would make Nella aware that Sofia needed to see the doctor.

'Fine.' Sofia cautiously hopped down the driveway on her own.

Holding back a grin, Antonio walked slowly beside her, passing the old cherry tree with its twisted trunk, and opened the front door for her once they finally reached it. After she had entered, he popped his head in. 'Nella, Sofia's sprained her ankle. She needs to rest and keep it up. I don't think it's broken but she has to get it checked.'

Nella leaned forward. 'Oh, my goodness! Are you all right, Sofia?'

Sofia sat next to her aunt and propped her foot up on a rush-seat stool. 'I'm fine.'

'Can you please make sure she calls the doctor?' asked Antonio.

'I'll call the doctor. I don't need *zia* Nella or anyone nagging me to do it.'

Nella raised her eyebrows at the same time as Antonio, and they shared a laugh. 'Anything I can do for you ladies before I go? Shall I organise some food for you for tonight? A potato or capsicum frittata?'

Sofia smiled and he wondered if she was finally warming to his attention. 'I'll be fine to grab some prosciutto and bread out of the kitchen later on, Antonio, thank you. We'll manage perfectly on our own, won't we, *zia* Nella? We're not completely incapacitated.'

Nella ignored her niece. 'Would you mind helping me walk to the bathroom, *Nino mio?* Sofia won't be able to take my weight in the state she's in.'

'No problem.' He lifted Nella off the bed and placed her next to it. Once she had her feet planted firmly on the floor, he escorted her, his arm around her waist, through the kitchen and down the corridor to the bathroom.

'I'll come by tomorrow morning, Nella, and hang around the whole day to help you out as Sofia will have to stay off her feet for a few days.' For a sprain. A broken ankle would be another story altogether, at least six weeks if that's what it turned out to be. 'I don't have anything planned and you can tell me all the gossip.'

Nella smiled gratefully at him. 'That sounds like fun, Antonio.'

Whether Sofia liked it or not, she wasn't in a position to do everything on her own for a while and he'd be damned if he didn't turn up when she needed him.

Sofia blinked a few times and let out her breath. 'If it's not too much of a bother, Antonio.'

'Not at all.'

She tilted her head and her lips curled up. 'It's very kind of you. Thank you.'

A warmth spread to his heart and he grinned. She'd accepted his offer, perhaps not at first, perhaps reluctantly, but she had let him in.

He'd be seeing a lot more of Sofia for the next few days and that was enough for him.

In fact, it was more than he'd dared hope for in a long time.

Chapter 4

Antonio stretched while he waited for his coffee machine to fill the cup he'd placed on it. The phone conversation he'd had with work the previous day at Nella's house played over in his mind.

Are you with someone?

Yes.

Able to isolate yourself enough so they don't hear me?

Yes.

Have you noticed any unusual activity?

No.

Stay close to home and be on stand-by in case there are any developments in the evening.

Tonight?

Yes. We've had a tip-off. Onorio and his men are on the move. They're supposed to be heading in your direction early evening. We don't know if they've located you or they're going somewhere else. So stay in tonight, OK?

OK.

Onorio. Matteo Onorio. Antonio was sick of hearing the name of the local Mafia figure who'd forced him into hiding.

As requested by his own superior, Antonio had stayed home the previous evening, and nothing had happened. He'd assumed that meant Onorio hadn't moved, that it had been a false alert, or that the trip in the direction of Sant'Agosto had been delayed. This morning, he'd checked his phone the minute he'd jumped out of bed, and still no sign of any trouble. He glanced at it again. Nothing there. No news was good news, wasn't it?

He grabbed his cup of coffee and shuffled over to his computer. There could be a message waiting for him on his PC. If there were any developments and details to be shared, he was more likely to receive the information through the computer. It was much harder to find someone through an IP address than to tap even the most secure phone.

He fired up his machine and took a sip of coffee, the strong liquid drawing the tiredness from his body. He was about to take another mouthful when his phone beeped. He pulled it out of his pocket, holding his breath. Writing lit up the screen.

No! It can't be!

He turned to his computer. It was the same there. Instead of the usual log on screen, three letters flashed intermittently. He stared at the message, three large red characters that chilled him to the bone: IPI.

IPI? *For God's sake, no!* When would the nightmare end? This couldn't be happening, not again. Not now that he was about to head out to see Nella. *To see Sofia.* The *Isolamento Pericolo Imminente* code—isolation due to imminent danger—meant that the Mafia was heading in his direction right now, this very minute, and all communication was prohibited until further notice. No phone. No computer. No leaving the premises. He had to go into hiding fast, close up the house so it seemed that no one was there, and lie low until he heard from the Commander himself.

He thumped his thigh. He could be in imminent danger lockdown for days, weeks even. He had to contact Sofia and let her know, otherwise what would she think? That he had promised to come and help her and Nella every day and then simply failed to turn up? That he didn't care enough to make the effort when both women were incapacitated and really needed him? She wouldn't put his absence down to an upcoming attack by the Mafia.

Last month, when he'd been shot and could have lost his life had he not rolled out of harm's way, it had been kept quiet. In fact, so quiet that the public didn't have an inkling of what had happened. There had been no mention of it in the media, and less than a handful of people in the ROS and the *Carabinieri* had had wind of the incident.

All that secrecy was beneficial, necessary even if you could swing it. It kept the population calm and avoided raising the profile of the Mafia, but it also meant there was no chance it would cross Sofia's mind that Antonio might have had to go into hiding because of such a threat, no chance that she'd put two and two together.

He took a deep breath, trying to steady his nerves. He was letting himself get carried away by the events. After all, he might only have a situation on his hands for a very short while. It could all be resolved in an hour or two. The procedure was clear: he was required to immediately lock up the home so that it seemed empty, closing the outside wooden shutters as well as all windows and doors, putting away his car and turning off all lights and any devices that could give away his presence. The vehicle was already in the garage, so he proceeded to pull shut and fasten all of the wooden shutters, as if the holiday home had been closed up for an extended period of time.

When he returned to his computer the screen had gone completely black. He pressed the Enter key, tried various other key combinations—to no avail. He'd been remotely locked out of the system. Shaking, he dug his phone out of his pocket and dialled his password, holding his breath. It was against the rules to contact anyone at this point and doing so could put him in serious danger, but if he still had a signal he was tempted to quickly call Nella and let her know that he couldn't visit for a while. He hesitated for an instant. What if the Mafia traced the call to Nella's place? Then she and Sofia would be compromised too, and he couldn't live with himself if they became Mafia targets because of him. No, he couldn't risk them being linked to him.

In any case, the decision wasn't his to make: while he pressed all the relevant keys the screen remained black, as if the battery had been totally discharged. The phone, too, had already been disabled.

He threw the useless device onto the coffee table. 'Merda!' He hated having to flee, having to hide and lie low. He hated not being in total control of his own life, even if he believed in what he did, believed in fighting the evil that penetrated every social layer of the country.

He clenched his teeth. Lamenting and protesting served no purpose. He couldn't override the system. There was no way to safely contact Sofia; if he did, he could be putting her and Nella in a perilous situation and he had to accept that, no matter how hard it was for him.

He threw himself onto the couch and held his head.

Someone might have tipped off Matteo Onorio as to Antonio's location and now the Mafioso was coming to get him and put a bullet through his skull, to make up for the one that only grazed him last month, and punish him for being the man behind Onorio's brother Salvatore's arrest which had landed the murderer in prison, waiting for his case to be heard.

Antonio went to the bedroom, unlocked his portable safe and took out his Beretta in case someone managed to find a way inside the house. He returned to the lounge room and sat on the couch, the gun by his side. He might be living his last hours, here, on his own.

He should be preparing to fight, saying his prayers in case it didn't go his way, writing a last letter to his family. He should be thinking of all the people who'd mattered over the years, all the places he'd been, and counting his blessings.

He leaned back on the couch and pressed his fingers against the cold metal of the gun. He wasn't afraid of the Mafia. He wasn't afraid to die. The only thing Antonio could think of was that he was letting down Sofia.

***

Sofia gasped, her whole body tensing with pain, as Doctor Linoni pressed her ankle.

'It hurts there?'

'Sure does.'

'And here?'

'Not as much. More like a bruise.'

'You are quite bruised, actually, much of it internally. How did it happen?'

'I jumped back on uneven ground to avoid a car that was coming fast.'

'And you twisted it inwards?'

'That's right.'

'When was this?'

'Yesterday.'

'Can you move it freely when you're not putting weight on it?'

'Yes.' She rotated it to show the doctor.

'And you can put it down a little?'

'I can put a tiny bit of weight on it. Not enough to walk properly, though.'

'I'm fairly confident it isn't broken. It's not impossible but it's rare that the bones around the ankle are broken or that a piece of cartilage is torn off with this type of injury, and you have all the symptoms of a sprain. We can do an X-ray if you like, to confirm my diagnosis, but I'd recommend giving it two or three days. If there's no improvement by then you'll definitely have to have it X-rayed to see the extent of the damage. Even if it isn't broken you could have an injury that requires attention, for example a small tear to a ligament.'

'If you're happy to wait, it's enough for me, Doctor. Let's see if it gets better on its own.' Besides, there wasn't anyone to drive her to the hospital in nearby Cassone, at least not yet. Where was Antonio? It was nearly lunch time and he hadn't turned up, nor bothered to phone. Her shoulders tensed. She couldn't rely on the General and that was fine. She didn't need to lean on a man and she should know better than to have expected him to do what he promised. So why the sinking feeling in her stomach?

'Be aware the bruising will worsen for a few more days,' added the doctor. 'Keep it elevated, rest as much as you can, put ice on it three or four times a day. A packet of frozen peas in a towel will do the trick if you don't have a proper ice-pack.'

'OK, I will.'

'You can take painkillers if you need to. If the level of pain worsens or hasn't improved in three days, I'll send you for X-rays.' The doctor turned to Nella, his expression kindly. 'And how are you feeling, lovely lady?'

'I'm better than when I was on the chemo. I can't lie to you, I still can't climb mountains, but I'm not twenty, either. A bit of weakness is to be expected, isn't it?'

'For sure. None of the signs we talked about?'

Nella shook her head.

'You get any of those, you go straight to hospital, *va bene*? We're lucky to have a nice new hospital nearby now. They'll take good care of you there.'

'I will, but I've had none of those symptoms. And no pain, either. Those tablets I'm on are miraculous.'

'That's good to hear.' Doctor Linoni stood and picked up his leather satchel. 'Shall I send Marisa over to help you out for a while, since you're both incapacitated?'

'No, Sofia and I are fine. Our friend Antonio's coming over. Antonio De Santis,' added Nella, eyes shining with pride.

Sofia pulled a face. 'He was supposed to come over two hours ago. Something tells me he isn't going to show.' He'd disappointed her before, showing his true colours in his youth. Why wouldn't he do the same now?

'Sofia!' Nella tutted. 'I'm sure he has a very good reason for being late and anyway, Marisa has more than enough to do at the office.'

'More than enough for *her*, although that doesn't mean much.' The doctor chuckled. 'If she wasn't my daughter, I'd send her off on her merry way. How did she turn out so lacking in enthusiasm? What did we do wrong?'

Nella giggled. 'You didn't do anything wrong. She's very young, that's all. Anyway, thank you so much for the offer, Doctor,' said Nella with a grateful nod. 'I'll keep it in mind but I'm sure Antonio will be here any minute. I'd have given you some fresh eggs, except that neither I nor Sofia are able to go and collect them. You're more than welcome to help yourself to them, if you like.'

'Don't worry about it, Nella. Sofia will give them to me another time.'

Sofia smiled her acquiescence. He probably didn't want to get his expensive shoes dirty by going into the chook pen himself, not for a few eggs, the only little present Nella was still able to give to those who visited. Not like in the good old days when Sofia's uncle was alive and he and Nella made delicious wine and honey and preserves and sausages and prosciutto and ... What hadn't they made together? People lined up for their produce.

Sofia pushed against her chair, ready to hop to the console where her aunt kept her purse. 'How much do we owe you, Doctor?'

He shook his head. 'Nothing at all, Sofia. I was here all of ten minutes and it's lovely to see you both. The truth is, I've been meaning to call in to check on you for a while, Nella, as a social call, and haven't had the chance. Shall I help you walk over to the bathroom before I leave?'

'No, I can still shuffle over to it *piano, piano* on my own most days and I'm feeling quite well today. So sweet of you to ask, though. May God watch over you, always.' She glanced up at the gold crucifix on the wall.

'And you. Anything you need before I go, Sofia?'

'No, I'm fine, thanks.' Nothing the doctor could do for her, in any case. The only thing that could calm her irritated nerves was Antonio finally making an appearance. She hated people who promised to help and then didn't.

The doctor waved before disappearing through the front door.

'Did you have to say that about Antonio?' asked Nella as soon as they were on their own again.

'Say what? That Mr Bigshot was supposed to come? It's the truth.'

'You told the doctor that Antonio isn't going to show. You don't know that.'

Sofia shrugged. What could she say to her aunt? That yesterday she didn't want Antonio to come over but today she had been waiting for him with bated breath? That his tardiness was slow torture, each passing minute more burdensome than the last? 'It doesn't matter, *zia*. I didn't want him to come over in the first place.'

'You know what I think, Sofia? I think you're upset that he isn't here, even if you don't want to admit it to me or to yourself. Why else would you pull a face like that when you told the doctor that Nino hadn't turned up?'

'I didn't pull a face, or if I did it was nothing more than a little annoyance. I don't like people who break their promises.' Like Terry, who'd promised to love and cherish her forever and instead had abused her trust, trampled her heart and served her a daily meal of belittlement, threats and fear on a silver platter. And for several years she'd kept that burden to herself, hidden under a cloak of self-blame and shame.

'Neither do I. Breaking promises is a terribly cruel thing to do.' Nella straightened the sheet that covered her legs. 'I don't like people who jump to conclusions, either. Do you? Life can be complicated at times and it isn't always possible to follow through with plans. You have to allow for that.'

'Hmm.' Sofia crossed her arms, settling further back in her chair. 'I also find people who are right all the time very, very annoying, *zia mia.*'

'I thought you'd be used to me by now.' Nella burst into laughter, throwing back her head.

For an instant Sofia saw the old Nella in her, the healthy, strong woman who was always waiting for an opportunity to tell a joke or play tricks, the fun country lady who brightened everyone's day.

It was a pleasure to watch, if only for an instant. Literally. Before Sofia could blink, Nella had settled back down and Sofia's mind wandered once again to Antonio, his absence, and his broken promise to come help them out.

She picked up the book she'd been reading and opened it, hoping to lose herself in the story for a while. It would stop her checking the clock every five minutes and take her mind off the General, and she desperately needed distracting from thoughts of Antonio.

***

The past few hours had ticked by slowly. Sofia had been unable to concentrate on her novel. The television hadn't held her interest either, and the conversation with Nella had been banal. Neither of the women had talked about anything much more personal than the weather, but their worries had filled the air with unspoken angst.

Sofia hobbled back from the kitchen where she'd managed to gather a light meal of prosciutto, cherry tomatoes, mozzarella cheese, walnuts and the sliced *pane di campagna* she couldn't get enough of, made from ancient grains and baked in a wood-fired oven. Thankfully the gigantic rustic loaf stayed fresh for a week or they'd be eating stale bread as neither Sofia nor Nella could go out shopping.

Sofia placed the plate on the small table next to her aunt, and sat on the other side of it. 'I didn't have the courage to stand at the stove to cook something tonight, *zia* Nella.'

Nella sat up. 'Goodness, I wouldn't expect you to, Sofia. This is perfect, and it must already have been a big effort for you to prepare it. Thank you. I'll clean up.'

Sofia giggled. 'You shall not. It's just two plates and two glasses, anyway.'

Nella munched on a piece of cheese and a slice of bread. 'It'll be easier tomorrow. Antonio will come over, I'm sure.'

A sound of annoyance escaped Sofia. 'How do you know that? He didn't even phone today. I mean, how hard is it to make a phone call?' She bit into a tomato, closing her eyes for an instant with pleasure as she savoured its full sweetness. Even simple food tasted amazing in Italy.

Nella scratched her chin. 'No, he didn't call, and it's not like him.'

'How well do you know this General? I mean, you saw him growing up, but since then? Not that often, from what I've gathered. People change, you know.' It was one thing to have a friendly chat with someone from time to time, quite another to rely on a person to help you out in times of trouble. 'It looks like we slipped his mind today. Completely. Maybe he isn't the reliable man you once knew.'

'He's a decent man, I know that much. And I mightn't have seen him for years, but I stayed in touch with his mother for ages. They're reliable people. There must be a good explanation.' Nella's brow creased with worry. 'What if ... what if something has happened to him? What if he had a car accident and we didn't even know?'

Sofia's stomach tightened at the thought. 'We would have heard, wouldn't we? The grapevine works rather well around here.'

'If you were chatting in town with someone, yes, they'd mention it. But who would think to call us at home?'

'Well, the doctor didn't say anything about an accident.'

'True.' Nella ate in silence for a while. 'Maybe Doctor Linoni's been busy with patients. I'd feel better if we checked with the hospital in Cassone. Shall we call them?'

Sofia nodded hastily and swallowed her food, the knot in her stomach tightening more, even if she made an effort to seem calm and disinterested. 'If you wish.' An accident hadn't been her first thought but now that Nella had mentioned it, Sofia, too, wanted to make sure Antonio wasn't hurt. If he was ... She didn't want to think about that because the minute she did, a knife twisted in her stomach.

She reached for the phone and dialled the number of Santa Maria di Grazia, her aunt's flash new hospital, the only one in the region. 'Hello. Has anyone by the name of Antonio De Santis been admitted today?'

Sofia held her breath as the receptionist checked. 'No, *signora.*'

She thanked the woman on the phone and smiled briefly at Nella, unable to hide the relief that washed over her. 'He's not there.' *Thank God.*

'That is good news.' Nella held up her hand. 'Before you accuse him of anything, let's hear what he has to say for himself tomorrow.'

Sofia gazed through the window at the falling night, the sky still tinged with an orange-pink that seemed to set the surrounding mountains on fire, and hoped that Antonio had a perfectly good explanation to offer, so that the darkness that was about to cloak the world didn't also spread to her heart.

She hadn't realised until then just how much she wanted to see him, despite their past, his absence today and her having given up on men. At least, most men. There might be an exceptional man waiting for her somewhere, mightn't there? An exceptional man like Antonio, or was that too much to ask?

Like a child, she crossed her fingers behind her back and with all her heart wished for Antonio to turn up in the morning.

Chapter 5

Antonio opened his eyes and listened. Birdsong in the garden. A couple of cars in the distance. A dog barking maybe three or four streets away. He reached down and found his gun on the tiled floor, exactly where he'd left it before falling asleep on the couch.

A tiny ray of sunshine filtered in through a crack in the thick wooden shutters, not nearly enough for him to see clearly inside the house. He switched on the lamp on the nearby desk and glanced around the lounge room: nothing was out of place. Was Onorio in Sant'Agosto now? Was he near Antonio, or worse, anywhere near Sofia and Nella?

He glanced at his phone. It was still off, so he made his way to the rustic bathroom and splashed cold water onto his face, some of the droplets wetting his shirt and falling onto the tumbled travertine tiles. He'd slept fully dressed on the couch, with his gun next to him, ready for action if the Mafia turned up on his doorstep. He was nearly disappointed that the night had gone by without disturbance because if Onorio had come for him it would all be over by now. Antonio would either be dead and have nothing more to worry about, or be free to go find Sofia.

Beautiful Sofia. She must be so angry at me.

Would she forgive him when he told her ... when he told her *what* exactly? What on earth was he going to say by way of explanation? The truth was out of the question; it would put her in danger. She couldn't know about Onorio and his attempt on Antonio's life, because if one day the Mafia should call upon her, ignorance was her best protection. *Merda!* This life of Antonio's played havoc with his plans, his passions, his relationships. It messed up everything that ever mattered.

Did Sofia matter to him? Clearly she did, even after all this time. She was all he could think about since yesterday, despite his own life being possibly at risk. All he wanted was to be able to contact her.

He returned to the lounge room and, annoyed, pressed the button on the side of his phone once more to check if it was operational again, but the screen remained black. He pressed the power switch on his computer too. Nothing. How long would he be incommunicado, a prisoner in his own home, at the mercy of his own safety, his own success, if you could call it that? What if he hadn't become the Vice-Commander of the special unit that was the

ROS? What life would he have led then? He'd sometimes wondered, but the question resonated louder than ever in his mind now. He thought back to that night on the balcony when he was just a teenager. What if Sofia had said yes? Would he be the same man today?

He wandered into the kitchen, made himself a strong coffee and sipped it, alone, his forced solitude weighing on his shoulders.

He'd much rather have shared his drink, his time, his mornings in Sant'Agosto with Sofia but he couldn't. At least, not for now and it pained him greatly.

***

Sofia washed the last dirty cup and placed it in the dish drainer hidden behind the country-style cupboard above the sink. She was thankful her ankle had improved tremendously overnight. It wasn't back to normal, far from it, but she was able to limp around the house and do the essential chores albeit gritting her teeth whenever she put too much weight on it. The doctor had been right, it obviously wasn't broken and that was a relief since she was the only one there to look after Nella.

Antonio certainly wasn't going to do it. Another day had gone by and still no news from him.

Traitor. Men are all the same. Disappointing one way or another.

She shouldn't have thought for an instant that there could be a man out there who was any different. She consciously loosened her shoulders as she wiped the plastic kitchen tablecloth. It was stupid of her to expect Antonio to do anything for Nella and her, totally unrealistic to expect the guy to stand by them, and the only one she should be annoyed with was herself. Why should he be devoted to her? They weren't blood relatives. They weren't married. They weren't even dating. And yet in her heart he somehow felt close to her, so very close. She couldn't deny that.

She splashed water around the sink, ridding it of the last of the dishwashing liquid and suddenly she was back in her youth, on a hot and sticky August afternoon. There'd been a storm so severe that the crystal clear waters of the river had spilled over gardens, mixing with the earth, and onto the nearby road, leaving dry only the middle of the bitumen and small islands here and there where bumps protruded. Antonio had happened to walk by while Sofia was out with her family—or had he been wandering around looking for her?—and she'd been so attracted by him, so distracted, too, that to go to him she'd stepped off the island where she'd found refuge and into the murky waters, ruining her new sandals and wetting a good part of her skirt.

Without hesitation he'd joined her, spoiling his pants, too, and they'd laughed about it before Sofia was called away somewhat sternly by her aunt.

She let out her breath, holding onto the sink. This was why Antonio still felt close to her. The memories.

The damn memories.

'Stop moping around and pass me the phone, will you?' Nella held out her hand.

'I'm not moping around.'

'You are and you've been doing a lot of it lately.'

Sofia huffed. 'Who do you want to call?'

'A friend, any friend, since you're certainly not chatty today. Maybe Adriana, if she's home.'

Biting her lip, Sofia handed the phone to her aunt. 'Sorry if I've been in my own little world.'

'Thank you, my darling. No need to apologise. It happens. Who else is in that little world of yours?' Nella suggestively raised an eyebrow.

'No one!' cried Sofia a little too forcefully. She turned away as she felt the heat rise in her cheeks.

Giggling, Nella dialled a number. She sat up straighter when someone answered. '*Ciao!* It's me, Nella. I'm fine, just fine.' Her eyes widened. 'Not *that* fine, Adriana.' She covered the phone with her hand so her friend couldn't hear her, and whispered to Sofia, 'She said I should join her for a swim if I feel good. Dearest Adriana.'

Sofia shook her head at the comment, before collapsing in an armchair, a magazine in hand. Nella wouldn't be exercising at the swimming pool for quite a while. For more than a while, actually, if things didn't turn out for the best. She wouldn't be exercising for ... forever. That wouldn't happen, would it? She wouldn't go and die on her?

Sadness wrapped itself around Sofia's stomach at the thought and pulled tight, like a python preparing its prey for consumption. Every now and then it slipped Sofia's mind that her aunt mightn't ever get better and whenever she remembered, it suffocated her. She reached out and patted Nella's hand. And then squeezed it with all her heart.

Nella smiled at her, tenderness in her gaze, as she continued on the phone. 'You're all well? The little one is better? Ah, that's good. I'm glad to hear it. Say, Adriana, would you mind doing me a favour? Would you go around to Nino's house to see if everything's OK?'

Sofia removed her hand from Nella's. What was her aunt thinking, involving someone else, asking them to go and check on Antonio? A sense of panic pushed up through her stomach and reached into her throat. 'Just leave it, *zia*. You don't have to send Adriana over there.'

Nella ignored her protests. 'That would be great, if it's no trouble. It's just that he was supposed to call in and he never did. I'm sure he's fine; he's probably tied up with work or something, but you never know. You haven't heard anything on the grapevine? No?'

Sofia rubbed her temple, keeping her head down once her aunt had hung up. Nella had done nothing wrong, Sofia knew that, so why was she upset about the phone call to Adriana? It was as if she were a teenager again, uncomfortable without really getting to the bottom of what bothered her.

'Spit it out, Sofia, or I'll nag you until you give in.' Nella's stern gaze told her that she meant it.

'I didn't want you to involve Adriana. Or anyone else, for that matter.'

'Because?'

'Because she has to go to the trouble of going to the General's place when she must have better things to do.'

'It's literally a few steps from her house.' Nella crossed her arms. 'The real reason?'

'That is the real reason. Oh, all right! The real reason...' Good question. Sofia took an instant to think about it. 'I guess I don't want people in town talking about Antonio and me as if we're a couple. Because that's what they'll assume. You know what they're like around here.'

'You're jumping to conclusions. They're more likely to simply think he's my friend's son, and that I'm worried about him. His parents used to visit me quite a lot, you know that, even if it was years ago. And anyway, so what if people think you and Nino are together? You're both adults and you're both free. I don't see the problem.'

Sofia shrugged. She couldn't answer her aunt in a manner that made complete sense. It was as if her feelings were getting in the way of her thoughts, confusion and disappointment wrapping themselves around her like a sheet thrown over her head.

'Well, then?' Nella's piercing stare forced her to delve further.

Sofia swallowed as clarity swept through her mind. *No more bad choices. No more mistakes.*

Next time, if ever there was a next time, it had to be the right man. Since the General could drop Nella and her the way he had, without even a phone call when he knew they were both incapacitated, he couldn't be the kind of man Sofia would take a chance on even if her heart beat faster when he was around. 'I won't be going out with him, so there's no point starting rumours.'

The shrill ring tone of the phone stopped Nella from asking more and Sofia sighed with relief. It was always good to be saved by the bell.

Sofia picked up the phone. '*Pronto?* Ah, Adriana, you've already been over there? That was quick.' She frowned as Adriana told her what she'd found at the holiday home.

'What is it?' Nella's eyes begged for information.

'All right, then. Thanks so much for doing that, Adriana. It will put *zia* Nella's mind at ease, I'm sure. You have a good evening. *Ciao, ciao.*'

She hung up and rested her neck against the back of the chair. The news had stolen the air from her lungs.

'What did she say?' asked Nella.

'The house is all locked up, the car nowhere to be seen. He's gone.' No goodbyes, no excuses. He'd left without a single word, disappeared into thin air like a thief without a conscience.

Nella leaned forward and patted Sofia's arm. 'It must be for work. Something urgent will have come up. He holds an important position, you know that.'

'Why wouldn't he have phoned us? He knew we were waiting for him. He could at the very least have asked his secretary to ring and tell us he'd been called away. Or phoned us while he was driving back to his office. Everyone has Bluetooth in the car now. That way he wouldn't have wasted an instant of his precious time on us.'

Annoyed, she let out her breath. And then Sofia shook her head as she recalled the telephone conversation he'd had the last time he was over, hidden away in the corridor so she and Nella couldn't see the expression on his face. *Yes.* Pause. *Yes.* Pause. *No.* Pause. *Yes.* Pause. *Tonight? OK.* He'd said it was work calling. Who spoke so little to their work colleagues? No names, no 'hi, how are you?' not one unnecessary word. What if it wasn't his office?

What if it was something he wanted to keep secret? What if it was a woman speaking? A woman who made him go weak at the knees, who made him go dizzy with excitement, so much so that he'd completely forgotten about Nella. And Sofia. The theory suddenly made as much sense as anything else. 'I need to get a bit of fresh air, *zia*. I'll sit outside for a while. Would you like a drink before I head out? *Acqua frizzante* with a slice of lemon?' Nella quite enjoyed the lightly sparkling water.

'No thanks, *cara mia*. You go ahead. I'll have a little rest.'

As Sofia was about to step out onto the patio, Nella called out to her. 'Sweetheart?'

'Yes?'

'I love you.'

'I love you too. And I like that you tell me so.'

The old woman chuckled. 'One day, a very nice man will say those words to you. You'll like it a whole lot more and it will warm my heart, whether I'm watching from down here or up there.' She pointed to the heavens above. 'You're going to be happy with someone. I know it.'

Sofia smiled sadly at the comment. 'We'll see.' She didn't have the heart to tell her aunt that she wouldn't bet on it.

***

Antonio had eaten his way through every packet of biscuits in the house, from the *frollini* with honey to the chocolate dipped almond horns, finished the book he'd been reading by the light of his small pocket torch and done more sit-ups, push-ups and bicep curls than he cared to count. Anything to pass the time. Anything to stop him from going crazy.

He glanced at his watch, thankful for the luminous dials that were easy to see even in low light conditions. It was ten to midnight. He ran his hand through his hair. Another day had gone by, hours trapped here without being able to contact the outside world.

Another day without Sofia.

Suddenly his phone and computers came on, beeping and flashing like the signs in Las Vegas. Antonio hurried to the nearest light switch and turned it on, blinking after the long hours spent in near darkness so that no light was visible to anyone outside the house.

He grabbed his phone, eager to dial Nella's number, but then scratched his head, sighing. She and Sofia would be asleep now, and he ought to find out first what had happened with Onorio and his men.

He dialled Carone, his Commander, on his personal phone number, the one only a handful of people knew about. He would answer, even in the middle of the night—he always did. Besides, he was most probably the person who had signed off on the assessment that the danger had now passed, giving the order to allow the reinstatement of Antonio's means of communication.

'*Pronto?*' Carone sounded wide awake.

'It's De Santis. My computer and phone have just been unlocked, presumably on your orders. I've been stuck inside my house here for over two days. What the hell's been going on?'

'Onorio and three of his men headed your way on Tuesday. They stayed ten minutes away from Sant'Agosto, in Vallerosa. The probability of them coming after you was high, so naturally we had to secure your person and property.'

'And now?'

'They've left the area. We're not sure why they were there, but it looks like it was something totally unrelated, a false alert if you like.'

'If I like? Are you kidding me? I do not like.' He'd blurted it out, when he'd never before spoken to his boss with such annoyance and irreverence. The fact that Onorio wasn't after Antonio didn't ease his mind in the slightest, even if he should have been relieved to hear that he wasn't in danger. All he could think about was Sofia and that he'd been kept from her for no reason. 'So I've been locked up going mad for a false alert?'

'May I remind you that Onorio nearly killed you last month and his men were ten minutes up the road from you? If it was up to me, I'd have sent you overseas for a very long time.

And you didn't even want to take an armoured car, for God's sake. I could have given you bodyguards.'

For what? So that they could get shot too? Antonio had seen that happen. Anyway, all the Commander could force him to do, according to the internal risk management policy, was step down for a while. 'You should be happy that I agreed to leave Rome. We're not even sure that they wanted to kill me last month. Maybe all they wanted was to scare me before Onorio's brother's case is heard.'

'Maybe, but we can't know that for sure.'

'Well, I've had enough of letting the Mafia rule my life and mess up my relationships, my friendships, everything ... People were expecting me two days ago to go and help them out and I couldn't even give them a call. People I care about.'

'Like it or not, you are the reason Onorio's brother has been handed over to the justice system. We had no choice but to put you in lockdown. What else could we do?'

Frustration rattled around Antonio's rib cage. 'You could have checked your facts. You could have asked me if *I* wanted to take the risk before you cut off all my means of communication.'

'Come on, you know that isn't the policy, De Santis.'

'Then, with all due respect, Commander, we should change the stupid policy.'

He'd said it as coldly as possible and had quietly put down the phone. The closing words in his mind that he had stopped himself from uttering were highly inappropriate and better kept to himself, and the fire in his chest that had been building over the past two days was ready to burn everything in its path. He'd been forced to stay inside, isolated from the world, isolated from Sofia, for no reason.

He'd let Sofia and her aunt down when they needed him.

He hated himself for it.

He opened his back door and stepped out into the garden. After two days staring at the ceiling, the sight of the starlit sky relaxed his core a little and he took a deep breath, the scent of the nearby jasmine vine filling his lungs. He concentrated on the warm breeze that caressed his skin, and he did his best to empty his mind.

He emptied it of everything except the one person he couldn't get enough of, the woman he wanted to see right now more than anyone or anything.

Now that he'd been kept away from her against his will, he knew.

He knew that he still needed her, that he wanted to try again with her, even after everything that had happened between them when they were young.

He'd go and find Sofia early in the morning and he'd fix things.

How? He had no idea, but he was sure that he had to, because she was meant for him, they were meant for each other. He could feel it in the pit of his stomach and in the way his heart fluttered just thinking about her.

That sense of belonging together was what had driven him to act the way he had all those years ago, and it was what was driving him back to her now. He closed his eyes and saw her face, the sweet face he'd nearly cupped in his hands the time they'd bumped into each other behind the church, the precious lips he'd nearly kissed. He'd chickened out and instead removed the petal that had fallen into her hair from the nearby oleander shrub.

He slowly let out his breath. Yes, he wanted her. He'd wanted her from the moment he'd laid eyes on her. Nothing had changed. He just hoped he wouldn't be quite as stupid about it this time around, and that she'd give him another chance.

If she did, he'd seize it with both hands and never let go.

Chapter 6

Antonio hesitated between the florist and the pasticceria. What would Nella and Sofia like best, cakes or flowers? What would be more likely to earn him their forgiveness? He decided to play it safe, that was, as safe as possible in the circumstances, and buy both.

'Can I help you?' The florist wiped her hands on her apron.

'I'd like a bunch of...' He stared at the red roses near the counter.

'These?'

I wish. 'No, thank you. Rather a mixed bunch. Something colourful. And a good size.'

'For a special occasion?'

Yes. I'm seeing Sofia. There's nothing more special. 'Just for friends, one of whom is sick.'

'Any particular colours?'

Which colour meant sorry? He didn't know and wasn't game to ask or the news that he'd done something wrong would be all over town. The joys of small communities! It was an aspect of life in Sant'Agosto that he hadn't missed while living in much more anonymous Rome, although there were plenty of aspects of small town life—the support, the friendliness, the sense of belonging—that he relished. 'I'll leave it up to you. Something elegant.'

'Right. I won't be long.' With a smile the woman busied herself, picking flowers out of the various buckets in the store and assembling them until she had created a stunning bouquet.

She wrapped a pretty ribbon around it and prepared to place a 'get-well soon' sticker on it.

'No!' Antonio held up his hand to stop her. 'Not the sticker.'

'I'm sorry, I thought you said it was for someone who was...' She'd probably realised as she spoke that Antonio meant his friend mightn't get better. Ever.

'It's really just to cheer them up.'

'I understand. Here it is.'

'It's beautiful, thank you.'

'No, thank *you* for doing what you do for our country. You're signore De Santis, aren't you? The Vice-Commander of the ROS?'

He smiled. The whole village had probably been talking about him being in town. 'I am and there's no need to thank me. I'm just doing my job.' He paid and made his way to the cake shop next door, a tantalising shop in a fittingly fancy building with a frilly, rounded awning that protected the shop window from the sun. There he bought a tray of sweet-smelling *cornetti*, his mouth watering as he breathed in the sweet vanilla scent, and escaped before the woman at the counter made a comment on his presence in the village.

As he climbed into his car his stomach churned but it had nothing to do with the *pasticceria*. How would Sofia react? Would she throw him out with his cakes and his flowers? Would she put an end to his hopes and dreams of a renewed relationship with her? There was only one way to find out.

He pushed his fears to the back of his mind, the way he did in his job, and drove, ready to face them head on despite the lump in his throat.

***

Sofia couldn't help but stare out the front window when she heard the low rumble of a car at Nella's gate. At the sight of Antonio's black hatchback, her heart fluttered. She huffed, annoyed with herself. She didn't want her heart to beat faster. Not for him. He didn't care enough to show up when he'd promised.

Nella sat up. 'Did I hear a car?'

Sofia grunted. 'The General has finally decided to grace us with his presence.' She watched him climb out of his Lancia carrying a huge bunch of flowers and a fancy package. 'And he comes bearing gifts.' As if that would fix everything. She pressed the remote to let him in through the gate.

'Oh, how nice of him!'

Sofia turned to her aunt. '*Nice?* Seriously, *zia,* after he didn't care enough about us to even call us?'

'*Permesso?*' His deep voice called out from the doorstep and Sofia hated herself for it but it sent a tingle to her core. His voice always had moved her, from the very first time they'd met when his parents had visited Nella and he'd come along. He'd said all of two sentences to her that afternoon while they sat under the vine-covered patio listening to the chirp of the crickets, but it had been enough to make her vibrate then, just as one word from him was enough to reach her now.

'*Vieni, vieni,* Nino,' answered Nella. Her face lit up at the sight of the huge bouquet that nearly hid his chest. Or was it simply because her golden boy was finally here? Sofia wasn't sure but her aunt's enthusiasm made her purse her lips.

He held out the flowers while Sofia pretended to be busy tidying what little was out of place: she straightened a few magazines left on the coffee table, moved this morning's mail from the console to Nella's inlaid wood desk.

Nella opened her arms to him, grinning ear-to-ear. 'Antonio, it's so lovely of you to bring flowers. Thank you. Sofia, take those beautiful flowers off Antonio, will you? And put them in a vase, please. You might need two vases by the look of it. It's such an enormous bouquet! I love the colours. So tasteful.'

He hugged the bedridden woman awkwardly, the flowers and boxed cakes still in each hand. 'It's for the two of you, flowers and cakes to say sorry for not being here.' He placed the box of cakes on the coffee table. 'I know you could have done with some help the past couple of days and I had every intention of coming over.'

Sofia tapped her thigh before daring to look him in the eye. 'It's true, we were counting on you. Don't worry, we managed just fine. Luckily my ankle wasn't broken.'

'I'm glad to hear that.' It would have been so easy to listen to the warm melody of his deep, masculine voice and forget all about everything else, everything he'd ever done, said, or perhaps more importantly not said, that had hurt her. But she knew better than to let anything quite so superficial sway her. She quickly turned her back on him.

He placed his hand on her arm and she shivered. She didn't want to, didn't want him to affect her that way. And she certainly didn't want him to see the impact that he had on her. She pulled away.

'I'm sorry.' His voice had dropped to nearly a whisper.

'We were worried about you.' Sofia threw him a sideways glance.

'That's true, we were,' added Nella rather casually. 'We even rang the hospital to see if you'd been admitted. Is everything all right?'

'Yes, no problem. Everything is fine. Something came up at work, something important and unfortunately I couldn't get away.'

Nella sought her niece's gaze. 'See, Sofia, I told you that was what it would be.'

'Well, thanks for the phone call to let us know, Antonio.' Fists tight, Sofia headed into the kitchen.

Antonio followed her in and placed the flowers on the tiled kitchen bench top. She stood at the sink, head bowed. How could he be so selfish, so nonchalant about it all? How could he care so little? She had been right to say 'no' to him when they were young. She'd wondered about it on more than one occasion, wondered if she'd acted impetuously with him as a teen and missed the love of her life.

Now she knew.

He wasn't worth it.

And still, her heart skipped a beat at the touch of his hand on her back, his fingers warming her skin through her blouse. She turned around.

His eyes were full of regret, and something else, something potent, mesmerising and deep. She couldn't put a name on it, didn't want to. 'I'm sorry, I couldn't call,' whispered Antonio. 'You have no idea how much I wish I'd been able to.'

'What? You lost your phone?' She looked away. She couldn't believe he was still trying to defend his actions.

'Yes, actually, for a while.'

'And you couldn't ask to use someone else's? Or even send me a message on social media? Better still, couldn't you stop by for a few minutes, a few seconds even, before you went off to God knows where to do your *work*, in response to that mysterious phone call you got at our house?'

'No, I couldn't. I had no way of contacting you. I get it, Sofia, I do. It all sounds so ridiculous. And here I am, asking you to simply believe what I say without proof or justification. Please believe me.'

Like God. She huffed. That was probably who he thought he was.

She filled the biggest vase Nella had with water and stuffed into it in the most inelegant way the bouquet that must have cost a fortune. 'You shouldn't have bothered. Flowers and cakes aren't going to get you back into the good books with me. I'm not that easily bought.'

Nella shuffled by, raising her eyebrows at Sofia.

'Zia! What are you doing up on your own? Let me help you.'

Nella waved her off. 'I'm going to the bathroom. I still have two legs. I just need to take my time.'

'I can carry you, if you like,' offered Antonio, opening his arms.

Nella chuckled. 'That won't be necessary. Just carry on the two of you, and ignore me.'

Sofia watched her aunt cross the kitchen and make her way down the corridor and into the bathroom.

When she turned back to Antonio, he was chewing on his lip. 'I can see that you're angry, Sofia, I can understand why and I'm very sorry. It was beyond my control. Maybe one day I'll be able to explain. But you know, perhaps it's karma.'

Karma? As if she deserved this? What the hell was he talking about? Sofia held onto the back of a chair as if she'd been dealt a blow to the stomach. A strong one. 'Excuse me?'

'I was so upset after what you did to me when we were young. Well, upset's an understatement. Devastated is more like it. Maybe we should start at the beginning and talk about that.'

Her head spinning, she grabbed a ladder back chair and hung onto it. If it hadn't been for the tick-tock of Nella's kitchen clock, Sofia might have thought that time had stopped. She followed the lines of the striped plastic tablecloth with her gaze while listening to the tap that dripped with painful regularity. Without warning, all her breath left her at once and anger took its place. Antonio was the one who'd jumped the gun back then, not her. She was at that party, a cousin's birthday celebration, standing on the balcony. He'd turned up unexpectedly, wearing a plain T-shirt and a scruffy pair of jeans, holding his helmet in one hand, and something small in the other. That something small had been a gift, a tiny box, one he'd casually thrown to her. *Thrown,* as if it had no importance whatsoever, as if he'd been aiming at a wastepaper basket, too lazy to walk over and dispose of his rubbish properly. There wasn't a girl in the world who dreamed of being treated that way.

But this wasn't just about dreams and fairytales. There was something much more important at stake. It was about building a relationship, and later a life, and to build something strong you had to be willing to put in the work. What did he know about Sofia back then when he'd decided to buy her that gift? If she'd asked him to write a list of what he knew of her that night, what would he have put on it? Hardly anything! The flavour of her favourite ice-cream, because as it so happened he'd bought her one at the *gelateria,* and maybe he'd simply guessed her preferences. Wasn't she worth spending time with? Didn't he care about discovering who she was? He'd never talked to her, apart from saying *'ciao'* once or twice or paying her a quick compliment, a superficial sentence here and there. The attraction between them was undeniable, irresistible, but he'd never made the effort or taken the time to *really* talk to her.

She sat, biting her lip, unable to glance up at him and yet she could feel his presence like the sun on her skin. She'd never been in the same room as him and not felt him. Her whole being had always come alive when he was near. Perhaps that was what had made his carelessness so cruel. She heard Nino clear his throat. Still, she kept her head down. He was upset about what *she* had done to *him* when they were young? How dare he!

As a young girl, she'd dreamed of Antonio. She'd wanted him. She'd had a longing in her loins she'd never known before, a heat in her core that had awakened her. But she hadn't realised until that very moment on the balcony just how little she'd mattered to Antonio, how little he'd been prepared to invest in her, to try to please her, to try to get to know her. She'd thought at first that something else was in the box. A pair of silver earrings. A cute pendant. Something to kick things off, to start the conversation that would be their life. Yes, the point from which everything would evolve and grow into a fruitful and meaningful existence.

When she'd opened the shiny package and seen the sparkling diamond ring, she'd thrown it back to him like a hot potato. She hadn't been able to comprehend exactly what it was. An insult? Provocation? A joke? The memory made her legs tremble and she was grateful she was sitting down.

She delved into her soul for the strength and control she needed to look straight into Antonio's eyes and say everything with dignity. Without wavering. 'No one gets engaged to someone they don't know. Unless it's an arranged marriage and I'd never have accepted one of those, even if we'd lived last century, Antonio. If you'd known me just a little you would have realised that.'

To decide to marry someone based solely on looks, on what you've heard of the family background, without first spending time together was ... pathetic. She shook her head with disappointment before continuing. 'It takes time to discover someone's soul and clearly it was an effort you weren't prepared to make, at least not with me. How could you have had any idea whether you were going to make me happy, or if I was capable of making you happy? You'd never even talked to me. I mean, not properly. You knew nothing of me, what I liked, what I dreamed of, what I hoped for out of life or who I was. And you definitely didn't know who I wanted to become. You know what really gets to me? It's the reason for it. It was because you just couldn't be bothered. Everything had to move along fast. Wham, bam, thank you, Ma'am. Is that what you wanted? Was it all a big game to you? It was so...' She frowned, digging deep into her feelings for the right word to describe them. 'It was so very *disrespectful.*'

Antonio's jaw dropped and he stared wide-eyed into nothingness, failing to defend himself. Then again, how could he, when he'd been absolutely in the wrong? Perhaps now that he was older, now that she was laying it all out before him, he could see that.

She took a deep breath. 'So, there you have it. Looks like you have nothing to say, huh?'

He rubbed his forehead for an instant. When his gaze met hers again she saw bewilderment in it. Bewilderment and pain. 'I'm flabbergasted.' His smooth chocolate voice had turned raspy. 'You've just dropped a bomb on me, Sofia. I always thought you felt the way I did, but I can see now that you were looking at things from an entirely different perspective. We were miles apart.'

She huffed. 'You can say that again. I get it, you were young, *we* were young, but a ring? A ring is about spending the rest of your life together.'

'I know that. Do you think I don't know that?' He came over to her, placed his hand on the table in front of her and leaned forward but neither with anger nor with harshness. It was more like a plea. 'God, I always knew that. But what you just said...' He shook his head. 'It was nothing like that.'

Suddenly screams from the bathroom pierced the air. 'No, no, no! Sofia!' Nella wailed with fear.

Sofia and Antonio ran to her. Thankfully she hadn't locked the bathroom door—she never did anymore just in case she had a bad fall and someone needed to come and rescue her.

Sofia turned to Antonio. 'It's best if you stay here. For privacy.'

He nodded. 'Of course. Call me if you need me.' He moved back down the corridor.

Sofia entered quickly, only to find Nella sitting on the toilet, a haggard expression on her pale face. She held out her hands covered in a thick, deep red liquid.

'*Zia!* You're bleeding! Goodness.'

A tear rolled down Nella's emaciated face. 'There are still things I want to see.'

'And you will,' said Sofia wishing she could believe her own words. 'They'll fix you up at the hospital, *zia,* don't you worry. It's not over yet. Are you in pain?'

Nella nodded. 'A little.'

'Shall I give you some painkillers?'

'No, it's bearable and they could interfere with whatever they'll want to give me in hospital. I have to wash, though. And I'll need those disposable panties. I think I still have a few in the cupboard there.' She pointed to the small cabinet that dated from the eighties. 'Or a flannel and fresh underwear will do. I keep some panties in there, too, so I don't have to go all the way back to the bedroom if ever I forget to bring some in when I take my shower.'

Sofia rummaged through the cabinet. 'Here it is.' She brought out the disposable underwear. 'Let's wash your hands and ... everything.'

The specialist had told them this could happen if things took a turn for the worst. Doctor Linoni had too. If cancer was generalised, the organs could deteriorate quickly. Could it have spread so quickly? Sofia didn't know, but rectal bleeding was one of the signs it was time to come into hospital. Time for heavy drugs.

Sofia pursed her lips. Was it nearly time to say farewell? God, she hoped not.

'I heard some of what you said to Antonio in the kitchen,' murmured Nella as the soapy water cleansed her fingers.

'You did? And I thought your hearing wasn't that good.'

Nella forced a smile. 'The old ears kick in from time to time. Listen, my sweetheart, don't be too hard on him, all right?'

'Don't you worry about Antonio. He's a big boy. He can fend for himself and you have more important things to think about right now. Like getting better.'

'Maybe...' She dropped her gaze to the floor. 'Maybe there is no getting better, Sofia.'

'You shouldn't jump to conclusions.' Sofia said the words as convincingly as she could, although it was hard not to think of the possibility of death. Nella would have to be a fool not to.

The ablutions over and Nella dressed, Sofia opened the bathroom door. 'Antonio?'

'Here.' He rushed to her.

'We need to get her checked out at the hospital. Would you mind helping walk *zia* Nella to the car?'

He smiled. 'I think I can do better than that.' He effortlessly scooped Nella up into his strong arms. 'We'll take my car. I'm parked behind Nella's Fiat.'

Sofia grabbed the small suitcase she'd packed for her aunt's emergency hospital stays, threw her own handbag over her shoulder and checked she had the house keys.

'Wait!' cried Nella as Antonio was about to step outside.

'Have you forgotten something?' he asked.

'Give me a second.' She looked around, gazing slowly, lovingly, at every piece of trusty sturdy furniture in the living room, every *bonboniera* a reminder of treasured weddings and births, every photograph of loved ones and special trips—to the canals of Venice, the ruins of Pompeii, and the stunning Amalfi coast not that far from home. She placed her hand on the wall, caressing it and the thousands of memories it held for her. 'Goodbye, my house. I've loved living here, you know, Antonio?'

'You'll be back.' His neck tightened so much that its tendons showed. 'I'll go settle Nella in the car, Sofia.'

'OK. I'll just be a second.'

He trudged up the driveway while Sofia locked the door, holding back the torrent of tears that threatened to roll down her cheeks.

Her stomach twisted with angst as she wondered whether Antonio was right. Would Nella be back? Did he say that to comfort her, or did he really believe it?

She wasn't sure. All she knew was that she wasn't ready to say goodbye to the woman who'd been a mother to her.

It hurt too much.

Thank goodness Antonio was here. Regardless of how he'd disappointed her by not turning up two days ago or how much his comment about their past had aggravated her, his presence comforted her now.

In fact, he was the one person, the only person, she wanted by her side now that her heart was breaking for Nella.

Chapter 7

Sofia sat back in the hospital armchair and relaxed. Her aunt was finally in peace in a comfortable bed, with a drip that dispensed medication directly into her blood. Nurses had been in and out, a doctor and his young intern had examined Nella and put Sofia's mind at rest as much as possible, and there was nothing left to do but try to recover from the events of the day.

Nella's eyes closed for a second before she forced them open again.

'It's fine, *zia*, don't fight it,' said Sofia patting the old woman's hand. 'You have a sleep. It'll help you feel better.'

'But you two are still here. I'm bad company and I don't want to be rude.'

Sofia smiled. It was sweet that Nella still thought about others in these circumstances. 'You're anything but rude.'

Antonio, who had been perched on a plastic chair on the other side of the bed, stood. 'It's time I went back, anyway. I probably have a pile of work waiting for me.'

'I'm sorry, Nino,' mumbled Nella, licking her cracked lips.

'You shouldn't be, Nella. I'm really glad I happened to be around this time to offer what little support I could.'

His gaze settled on Sofia, his warm, apologetic gaze. He was trying to say sorry for not being with them over the past few days, wasn't he? How could she stay mad at him? She couldn't, not for that. But for blaming her for what had gone wrong between them when they were young, oh yes, she ought to resent that for a long time even if she was having trouble holding onto the dismay his comment had brought her. She'd do well to remember how it had made her feel. If only he'd stop looking at her that way.

He patted his pocket, checking for car keys. 'I can pick you up later, Sofia, if you like, since I drove you here. What time will you be leaving the hospital?'

'No need, thanks. I'll catch a cab, but I can walk you out. I want to drop into the cafeteria anyway. Shall I bring a drink or something to eat for you, *zia* Nella?'

'I'm fine now, *bella*. You see to Antonio. In fact, why don't you go home with him?' Her heavy eyelids closed once more, tighter this time. 'The nurses will look after me. And I'm falling asleep, anyway, so I won't be good company.'

They quietly left Nella's room without answering as she dozed off. Sofia and Antonio walked side-by-side down the corridor to the lift, their eyes on the floor. Sofia pressed the green button and watched the lights change as the lift descended one floor after another.

Antonio cleared his throat. 'Shall I take you back to Nella's, then?'

'No, I'll stay even if she's asleep. You never know. She might wake up and need me.' She didn't want to be away if things went wrong. She especially didn't want to be away in her aunt's final moments. She hoped the time hadn't yet come but there was no way to be sure of that, not yet.

He nodded. 'How about I hang around, then? I only said I had to go home because Nella seemed to feel bad about dozing off with me sitting there.'

Sofia held her stomach as the lift opened before them. She stepped inside and Antonio followed. There, in the small space, she breathed in his cologne and her heart pounded in her chest. They were alone, so close that all she had to do was lean forward to place her head on his shoulder.

She'd feel his skin against hers, she could even kiss him if she dared. Her heart screamed 'yes'. Yes, even if Antonio hadn't turned up to help her and Nella out when he'd promised and hadn't bothered to call and tell her why, or at least make an excuse. Yes, even if he'd said he should be angry at her for not accepting his ring back when they were so young they barely understood the deep implications of such a gift.

She steeled herself, quickly leaning away from him. Holding onto the metal handrail, she pressed level '0'. She didn't have to listen to the song her body was singing. She could stick to reason, couldn't she? Her head said 'no'. Antonio wasn't right for her. No man was. She looked up at him. There was sadness in his lopsided smile, sadness and longing and desire.

She sighed. He'd helped her today and she was so very grateful for his presence over the past few hours. Whatever it was that she felt standing there next to him, in that lift, just the two of them, the thing that sped up her heart and made her aware of her body more than she'd ever been, was stronger than anything she'd ever experienced.

Damn it. I can't send him away.

She quickly pressed level '1' just before they arrived at the floor the cafeteria was on. 'Let's have a coffee. If you'd like to, that is.'

He smiled with the eagerness of the teenager she once knew and it warmed her heart, just like it used to. 'That would be nice.'

The lift stopped with a clunk, the floor bouncing slightly under Sofia's feet. As the doors opened, Antonio placed his hand on the small of her back and she shivered before stepping out in front of him, hoping he didn't notice the effect he still had on her.

***

Antonio sipped his coffee without taking his eyes off Sofia. The poor woman was a ball of nerves after having to hospitalise her dear aunt. Now wasn't the time to continue the discussion they'd been having when Nella had cried out in pain, no matter how much he wanted to defend his actions as a teenager. No, not defend them. *Explain* them. Because it was obvious to him now that Sofia didn't understand why he had acted the way he had when they were young.

Sofia quietly drank her apple juice, following the imitation wood grain on the melamine table with her index finger.

Antonio glanced around the otherwise empty cafeteria, checking it for danger as he did every public place, before letting his gaze settle on Sofia again. 'I'm glad Nella's comfortable now,' he ventured.

Sofia's eyes met his for an instant. 'Me too.'

'This is a good hospital, brand new, and I saw in the press that they had managed to attract top staff. They'll look after her well.'

'Yes.' She tilted her head. 'Thanks for helping. I appreciate it.'

'My pleasure.' It would be his pleasure to do anything for Sofia. Anything she wanted.

They sat in silence for a moment.

'I think we should talk about—' he said.

'We ought to talk about—' she blurted out at the same time.

He smiled. Thank goodness they were thinking along the same lines. 'The elephant in the room?'

She nodded, averting her gaze. 'Now that we finally have the time to talk.'

'I wanted to earlier but it wasn't the place in the hospital room, with Nella's condition being possibly so serious.'

'You're right, the hospital room wasn't the place to continue the discussion, although that isn't what I meant. What I meant was, we have a chance to say what perhaps should have been said all those years ago. I know there are things I should have said sooner.'

He blinked, trying to focus on her words and not the sensation that an invisible person was pressing a fist into his chest. 'I'm listening.'

'OK then.' She tapped the table lightly as if searching for her words. 'You followed me around plenty when we were teens, checking me out, but you never took the time to get to know me. You never spoke to me. And that's OK if it's the very beginning of a relationship and you follow it up with a stage where you do get to know the person. But that night on the balcony, you threw me a ring, and it made me feel so unimportant, so unworthy. It made me feel like I didn't matter enough for you to find out what made me tick before you decided to get engaged. To be truthful, that night I felt like it was all about ... How can I say this? My appearance. You obviously wanted someone for their looks, because that's all you knew of me. And I wasn't cut out to be a trophy wife. I wasn't even ready to become someone's fiancée.'

'Your appearance?' He sighed. The accusation was like a knife to his stomach. 'It wasn't like that, Sofia. Not at all. Yes, I admired your body, who wouldn't have? You were so very beautiful, the most beautiful woman in the world to me, and you still are, but that wasn't the reason. You said earlier that I was disrespectful. You have *no idea* how much I respected you.'

She let out a sound of surprise. 'OK, well, if that's respect, I just don't get it. You didn't seem to agree with me when I told you I felt it was all a big game to you and that you just wanted things to move along fast. Just before Nella screamed out in the bathroom, you were saying that it was nothing like that. So help me out here. It's your turn to explain yourself.'

He wanted to wrap his arms around her and hold her against him. He wanted her to feel what his heart felt, what his whole body felt, every time she was near. Perhaps then she'd understand. 'It wasn't that I couldn't be *bothered* talking to you, Sofia. It was that I *couldn't* talk to you, no matter how hard I tried. I was young and terribly shy, and you had such a huge effect on me. Before you, I had no idea such a feeling even existed, let alone think it could happen to me, a kid who was nobody. I so wanted to talk to you and every evening I went over and over what I'd decided to say. I had entire conversations with you in my head. I was so clever in them, in my imagination. I rehearsed in front of the mirror. My dad thought I was going crazy. Still, every time I saw you I became incapable of putting two words together.'

You mattered so much. More than anything.

She chuckled and it gave him hope, hope that she had caught a glimpse of the real man in front of her. 'If I didn't talk to you, Sofia, it was because you dazzled me, like the sun. You robbed me of all of my words. I was in awe of you. Didn't you know that? I thought it was so obvious.'

She hid her face in her hands for an instant before holding onto the edge of the table. 'No. I honestly had no idea. I ... Oh, God. I guess I was young too. I thought you didn't care enough to want to learn who I was, to find out if we'd be good for each other, if we were a good match.'

'A good match? Wow. I didn't need to talk to you for that. What I felt was so strong, I just knew. It wasn't because I didn't care that I was paralysed when I saw you. It was because I cared too much.' It had been stronger than a certainty from the minute he'd laid eyes on her. It went far beyond words and fancy sentences, straight to his soul that reached out to hers. She was meant for him. He could sense it the way you sense a stranger behind you in the dark. There was no logical explanation, nothing but a deep perception of the truth.

You were my faith.

Their eyes met and it sent a ball of warmth to his stomach. 'You were the first person I felt so strongly about. And...' He took a deep breath and then another.

'And?'

'It's never been like that with anyone since.'

Sofia's eyebrows shot up. 'But you've been married.'

'And divorced, obviously for good reason.' The only person he ever should have married was sitting right in front of him.

Sofia placed her hand on his forearm. 'You said before we left for the hospital that you were devastated after what I did to you. You want to talk about that?'

He hesitated. What he had to tell her would displease her but she needed to hear it and, after carrying it around in his heart for so many years, he owed it to himself to get it off his chest. He swallowed hard. 'I'd worked that summer and saved all my money. I'd agonised over rings, spent hours in front of jewellery stores. The day I finally found one I thought was lovely, as lovely as you, and the best one I could afford,' he said with a chuckle, 'I bought it and went looking for you. It was an impulse and I felt so happy I thought my heart was going to burst. When I saw you on the balcony that evening in town, I told myself it was my moment. It seemed romantic at the time. It reminded me of Romeo and Juliet.' He laughed bitterly, at the memory, at himself, at how wrong he'd been, before continuing. 'But you threw the box back at me without a single word.'

Like a piece of rubbish. Like *he* was rubbish. 'You broke my heart, Sofia. You really did.'

For a while, she'd broken his spirit too, until he'd decided that he would prove her wrong. He'd study, he'd work until he dropped, but he'd prove his worth. He'd impress those around him. And one day, he'd impress *her.*

She rubbed her forehead. 'I'm sorry. I'm sorry it didn't work out back then. For both of us. How did we manage to understand each other so little?'

He shrugged. 'We were barely more than kids. We had a lot to learn. Things were bound to go wrong.' But they weren't immature anymore. Maybe now that it was all out in the open, they could start afresh.

'I guess we were too inexperienced.'

They sat in silence for a while and then Sofia's stomach rumbled loud enough for Antonio to hear it. 'You're hungry?'

She nodded. 'Yeah, but I'm not that keen on the meals they serve here. How about we go somewhere else and get something decent to eat?'

A man entered the cafeteria and Antonio studied him. One metre seventy-five. Late fifties. A noticeable limp and a worried expression. He was unlikely to be a member of organised crime.

'Antonio?' Sofia raised an eyebrow.

'Sorry? You were saying?'

'It's twenty past one. Shall we go out to get a bite to eat? We could go to the pizzeria up the street. What do you say?'

In public, with Sofia, when the Mafia had been in the area the past couple of days? Was it wise? He hesitated. It was in a nearby village, not here in Cassone, that Onorio had been spotted, and now he and his men appeared to have left. The risk had passed, hadn't it?

Antonio smiled. 'I'd love to.' He looked into her eyes, those amazing eyes he could drown in, and his stomach turned inside out.

His hunger was for Sofia.

***

The sun warmed Sofia's back and it loosened as she and Antonio walked the short distance that separated the hospital from the pizzeria, passing yellow and white square buildings with washing hanging from every second window and a dense collection of satellite dishes on the flat roof that must have looked like a field of giant mushrooms from the planes that flew above. She suspected the heat wasn't the only reason the tightness in her body had left her. Knowing that she'd mattered so much to Antonio all those years ago filled her heart with peace, and perhaps more importantly with renewed hope and greater faith in the opposite sex.

God knew she needed hope and faith after her rotten marriage to Terry.

It wasn't because Antonio didn't care. It was because he cared too much.

He'd cared when he'd sat beside her in her aunt's garden and whenever he'd smiled at her from a distance. He'd cared every time he'd followed her around on his Vespa and when he'd bought her gelato. He'd cared the night he'd walked by her side all the way up the hill behind the procession for the *festa* of Santa Maria del Carmine, and he'd definitely cared when he'd saved up his birthday money, his Christmas money and what he'd earned from holiday jobs, to buy her a ring. Now that she understood it, she couldn't resent him for anything that had happened.

Not like Terry who never gave a damn about her. It was all about satisfying his every whim, all about his power over her. It was all about *him*.

Not with Antonio. He'd always cared for her.

Just the way she had for him. It was as if she'd finally discovered the meaning of life itself, and she wanted to jump up and down and scream it to the world, her heart about to burst with the deepest joy she'd ever experienced.

He cares about me! He really cares.

She slipped her hand around the crook of his arm and grinned, pulling him a little closer. 'So how does it feel to be back in Sant'Agosto?'

'It's really good. Rome is exciting and full of life and I like that too. Sant'Agosto is...' He came even closer to her, his hip brushing against hers as their steps synchronised. 'Sant'Agosto is so much better because it's where you are.'

She laughed, although she wasn't making light of his statement. Quite the opposite, it brought her true happiness. 'I love Rome, the fountains, the ancient buildings. Actually, I could see myself there.'

His eyes widened with surprise. 'You could?'

'Maybe one day.' *Especially because you're there too.*

'What's Australia like?'

'Beautiful. A land of sunshine and freedom. The earth is really red, the sky is really blue and with the people, it's what you see is what you get. It's far away from the rest of the world, though.'

'It sounds wonderful. Even the remoteness.'

He placed his hand on the small of her back as they arrived at the pizzeria, a charming stone building with corbels around the windows, and guided her to the arched door. She liked it, how his fingers felt against her, the closeness, the promise of more to come.

A waiter approached them. 'Buongiorno. A table for two? Inside or outside?' The restaurant was lucky enough to dispose of a large outdoor eating area that must have been converted from a prior courtyard.

'Let's sit out the front and watch the world go by,' suggested Sofia. She wanted to while away the hours the way the Italians did, in the shade of the colourful umbrellas that adorned every outdoor table. She couldn't—she'd have to head back to the hospital soon—but she'd thoroughly enjoy whatever little time they had together on that sun-drenched terrazza.

'Hmm...' Antonio cleared his throat. 'I'm not a big fan of being in the open.'

'Why not?' Sofia squeezed his arm. 'Oh, come on, it's a perfect day for it. A table outside, please.'

'Si, signora.' The waiter showed them to their seats and offered them menus.

Antonio sat with a sigh and a frown on his face. Since when didn't he like being outside? 'Do you remember sitting in the garden with me at Nella's when we were teens?'

'I do.'

'The time we counted the stars for ages?'

His lips curled into a dreamy smile. 'I'll never forget it.'

'You were a fan of sitting in the open then.'

'I thought that spending time outside under the stars was my best chance of getting a kiss from you.'

'Oh, well, if you're very nice to me, I might kiss you out here in full daylight.'

'In that case, I'll be on my best behaviour.' He chuckled and they chose their pizzas—a *siciliana* and a *quattro stagioni* —also ordering a glass of Chianti each to wash them down.

Antonio leaned back against his chair and studied her. 'You're more beautiful than ever.'

She placed a strand of hair behind her ear, fire rising in her cheeks. 'Thank you. You're not bad yourself, if I may say so, General.'

He let out a hearty laugh. 'General? I'm not a General. Why did you call me that?'

She shrugged. 'It's your nickname around Sant'Agosto. Everyone's so sure that you'll be promoted to that very honourable level very soon.'

He laughed even louder. 'Well, I wouldn't be so sure. I suppose it's a lot better than many other things they could call me.'

'Like what?' She giggled with him, his laughter infectious. And she loved that little dimple that formed in his left cheek when he let go.

'Let me think. How about Mr Pig-head? I've heard they call the police pigs in some countries, don't they? The *carabinieri* are close enough to the police, so that would fit. And it would make a nice reference to my stubbornness too. Or how about the Nutjob? After all, I did crash my Vespa for no apparent reason when I was a teen. Do you remember that?'

She laughed harder. 'I sure do. You drove by staring at me the whole time until you swerved and went flying onto the grass next to the road. Thank goodness you weren't going fast. My heart stopped for a second and then you jumped to your feet, gave me a thumbs up and drove off as fast as you could.'

'You can't blame me for being embarrassed. You and I are the only two people who know the whole thing happened because I couldn't take my eyes off you. Everyone else to this day thinks I was off my rocker when that happened. Half of them probably still do.'

'You are definitely not a nutter.' If anything, she'd been the crazy one to not understand how lovely he was. She shrugged teasingly. 'Maybe you are and you're hiding it from me.'

Before she could check Antonio's reaction to the banter, the waiter came over, one pizza in hand, the other resting precariously on his arm, and served them. Sofia nodded her thanks and picked up her knife and fork to dig into the food that smelled delicious. *'Buon appetito."*

When she looked up at Antonio he was staring at something in the street. She followed his gaze to ... to what exactly? There was nothing there, just a row of cars parked along the road, as always, as close as possible to the narrow footpath on the other side of the road. 'Antonio?'

He turned his attention to her, his expression suddenly harsh. 'Let's go to my place.'

'Excuse me? We've just been served our food.'

'I have plenty in my fridge,' he said more forcefully. 'All I have to do is heat it up.' He stood.

A sense of panic rose in her at the drastic change in his behaviour. 'We're here to have lunch and then I'm heading back to the hospital. *Zia* Nella might wake up and I want to be there in case she needs me.'

'Just do as I say.' He wrapped his fingers around her arm. 'Come with me. Now.'

She shook his hand off her. 'What on earth are you talking about?'

'Please don't make a fuss.'

She raised a hand, and the waiter came over. 'Something's come up,' she blurted. 'Would you mind packing my pizza for takeaway?'

'*Subito, signora*,' said the young man as he picked up her plate. 'This one too?' he asked, pointing to the General's pizza.

Antonio handed him a banknote and waved him off like a fly buzzing around his dish. 'Keep your head down,' he ordered, tugging at Sofia's arm and dragging her away from the restaurant before the waiter had the time to return with her packed pizza and the change. 'We're in danger.' As he escorted her out, past three men in suits who were arriving, Antonio held her close, with a strength that surprised her, and with his free hand he buried her face against his chest.

A few metres up the street Sofia stopped, freeing herself from him with a tug. 'What was all that about? I see no danger. We were in a restaurant eating pizza and suddenly you did a Dr Jekyll and Mr Hyde on me.' She cast her mind back to what they'd been saying when he changed. She'd teased him about perhaps being a nutter and hiding it well. Was that what had set him off?

'Let's keep going.' He placed his hand on her back, encouraging her to walk.

'When you've told me what the hell is going on.'

'You don't need to know.'

'What? I'm too stupid to understand?' She raised an eyebrow and leaned towards him.

'No, Sofia, it's not like that. It's just, the less you know, the safer you are.'

'Don't you think that's rather convenient?' She huffed and took off, marching up the street at a good pace. She'd had it with men who tried to keep her in the dark.

Antonio threw his hands up in the air, striding next to her while she hurried, his legs so much longer and faster than hers. 'OK! The men, those men that were coming into the restaurant...' He sighed, running a hand through his hair.

She stopped for an instant, turning to him. 'Talk to me, Antonio. They're Mafia? Is that it?'

'I can't say that for sure.'

'You can't or you won't?' He looked away. 'Right. Have it your way.' She started up the street again while he followed her like a little dog.

Around the bend, the square grey outline of the Santa Maria di Grazia Hospital came into sight. 'I'm going back to sit with Nella.'

He placed his hand on her shoulder. 'You'd be safer somewhere else. Come with me to my place. I can keep you hidden there.'

'Not a chance in hell.' He wouldn't even tell her who those men were, and he wanted her to follow him blindly. And what about Nella? 'There's no way I'm leaving my aunt when she needs me most and...'

'And?'

Sofia let out all the air in her lungs. She'd had it with bossy men. 'And I do what I want.'

'OK, you do what you want, but listen. Let's not make a fuss in the open air and just get ourselves to the hospital.' His brows joined up in the centre to form one furrowed line while he shoved his hands into his pockets. 'Actually, you go ahead.'

'So now I'm in danger but you're not coming with me?' Her stomach tightened. Was he the type to disappear the minute they had the slightest disagreement, to run as soon as there was a hiccup?

They reached the entrance to the hospital grounds and entered the carpark. Antonio glanced behind them and down the street. 'It's better if we're not seen together so I think I'll leave you here.'

She studied him for an instant. He seemed older now that his face was creased with worry. She couldn't decide whether he was overreacting, or whether they truly were at risk. 'Fine. I'll be by Nella's side if you decide to come and see me.'

'You're not going to the cafeteria first?'

'I've lost my appetite. You haven't?'

'Hmm, yes. There's food at home anyway. I should probably just ... go.'

'Up to you.' She made her way to the double doors to the building that parted automatically when she approached them.

She paused before walking in and turned around, checking behind her, but her shoulders slumped with a mix of disappointment and annoyance.

Without further explanation, Antonio had disappeared.

Chapter 8

Antonio slipped behind a concrete pillar as Sofia glanced over her shoulder. He'd followed her at a good distance, not wanting her to kick up a fuss about him being there and draw attention to them. Because that was exactly what she would do if she realised he hadn't gone home like she thought he had. If she knew he was around, she'd come looking for him, she'd talk to him, perhaps argue with him and that might result in him being seen with her. Clearing off and leaving her alone wasn't, however, an option for Antonio: there was no way he would walk away from her when Onorio's men might be just down the road. The only thing he could do was make her believe that he'd gone home but stick around and defend her if the Mafia went after her.

His mission required the greatest care, though. They were exposed enough as it was. One slip-up and Onorio's men could very well notice the unexpected shadow behind Sofia and find him—and more importantly Sofia—that way. Organised crime trained its members to spot any unusual behaviour and to look more closely. He rubbed the top of his left arm where the bullet had grazed him the last time he'd come eye-to-eye with Onorio. Luckily, his body had instinctively remembered the days when he'd been more active on the field and less confined to a fancy office, and he'd rolled out of harm's way. Well, nearly. He had a flesh wound, a superficial one. Perhaps the damage to his psyche had been greater.

Now what mattered, the only thing that mattered, was keeping safe the woman who made his heart beat. Still. After all these years. He hadn't expected to feel so much for her so soon, but he did. It was all there, intact, hidden under the shield that the years had formed, and he'd gladly risk his life to protect her even if she hated him right now. Just when things were going so well between them. He bit his lip. Had he ruined everything with her? He hoped to God that he hadn't.

Sofia set off again, her hair bobbing up and down more than usual with the force of her irritated steps. She pressed the green button to call the lift, and stepped into it as soon as it opened. Antonio would take the stairs, run up them two by two, and be right behind her in the corridor that led to Nella's room when she reached the second floor.

He checked behind him, letting out his breath when he saw no one suspicious, just a woman with a baby in her arms. If Onorio's men spotted him and saw that he was following someone, they might come to realise that for him do so, for Antonio to risk them finding him instead of going into immediate hiding, the Vice-Commander of the ROS cared about the person very much.

He had to avoid that at all costs.

He rubbed his forehead. His office had told him that Onorio and his guys had left the area, that it had been a false alert when they were spotted in a nearby village days ago. According to his superiors, Onorio's men didn't appear to be looking for Antonio. But the three somewhat shady characters who'd walked into the pizzeria earlier looked familiar. Were they part of Onorio's gang?

Antonio had a niggling feeling that they were. He was sure he'd seen the face of the tallest one somewhere, possibly a mugshot or a secret service file. Or had the guy been there the day Antonio was shot? He closed his eyes for a second, concentrating on that moment. The wrong food had been delivered to his office that day. Antonio was allergic to pine nuts, and so couldn't eat the ricotta, spinach and pine nut pasta before him. To buy a more suitable meal, he'd stepped outside on his own, on foot, something he hardly ever did, and they'd been waiting for him in the bustling street, blending in with those who stood in line to buy a slice of pizza or a steaming *calzone*.

As he climbed the stairs, he remembered the sound of the bullet whistling through the air that day, the hate on Onorio's face. Three men in the background. No matter how hard he tried, he couldn't visualise their features, damn it. It had all happened too fast.

But if the men at the pizzeria today were part of Onorio's gang, why hadn't they killed Antonio by now? What were they doing here if not looking for him? Or was he imagining things, and the men he'd seen when out with Sofia were nothing more than customers of the pizzeria?

He'd been shot last month and had refused the counselling offered to him. Was he suffering from paranoia? Post traumatic stress?

Too many unanswered questions. He didn't like it. It certainly felt like he was going crazy.

He reached the second floor and stood behind the door that led from the stairwell to the corridor, opening it just a crack. The ping of the lift sounded, and he caught a glimpse of Sofia as she made her way back to Nella's room.

He gave her two minutes to make it to her aunt's side before he cautiously stepped into the corridor, checking in both directions that Onorio's men weren't around. The door to Nella's room was still swinging—Sofia was probably in there, although he'd learned not to assume anything. He walked up to it, making an effort to keep to a normal pace rather than chase after the woman he wanted to keep safe at all costs, and glanced through the small rectangular glass pane in the door to room number 213. Perhaps Sophia sensed him: she looked in his direction.

'*Merda*,' he mumbled before jumping out of the way. Had she seen him? Would she come out to make sure she wasn't imagining things? There was a good chance she would. He checked his surroundings. There was nowhere to hide, except...

He rushed into the next room and greeted the patient with a smile. Antonio stood in the corner of the room, on the same side as the door so he couldn't be seen from the corridor, in case Sofia peered through the glass, looking for him.

He eyed a card on the patient's bedside cabinet. *Dear Mario,* it started. That had to be the old fellow in bed, staring with his mouth open at Antonio. 'Mario, it's so good to see you.'

The patient sat up. 'Do I know you?'

'Do you know me?' Antonio laughed. 'The medication people are on in here can have certain unexpected effects, but do you know me? It's *me*. You don't recognise me?'

Antonio caught his breath as footsteps resonated in the corridor before stopping in front of the room. Suddenly, the door opened and Antonio retreated even further into the corner, if that was possible.

'And who are you, now?' snapped Mario leaning forward even further in his bed.

'I'm sorry, I've got the wrong room.' Sofia's words floated through the air while Antonio held his breath, praying that she didn't enter.

The door closed, and Antonio let out a sigh of relief.

'I don't know who that one was, either,' mumbled Mario. 'Pretty thing, though.'

Antonio smiled at the comment and stepped forward. 'Well, I'm glad you're looking so much better, Mario.'

'How so? I haven't had the operation yet.'

'Really? Then I must go and tell off those doctors for keeping you waiting. Bye, now.'

'Wait a minute. Who are you? How do I know you?'

Antonio slipped out. There were a few chairs further up the corridor. From there he'd be able to see anyone suspicious entering Nella's room and get to it quickly to protect Nella, to protect Sofia. He should have the time to slip into another patient's room, too, to hide the minute Nella's door swung open, before Sofia appeared in the corridor again—the chairs were close enough to yet another hospital room.

And while he couldn't talk to his office on the phone for fear of being overheard, he'd send a message to find out if there was any news about the whereabouts of Onorio and his men.

He'd much rather be by Sofia's side right now, holding her hand, seeing her eyes light up whenever he said something that struck a chord with her, but for the time being watching her from afar was the best he could do.

Antonio typed a text to the woman he trusted the most in the professional world, his right hand, Gina Norello, glancing up every word or two to make sure no one snuck unseen into Nella's room.

Is Onorio back in this area?

The response came almost immediately. *No, we would have warned you.*

His men?

Same. No suspect in your area or heading your way. Why?

Trust Gina to ask why. Nothing ever went unnoticed with her. And she never let anything go, either. She dug until she had all answers, until everything was crystal clear. Tenacious was her middle name. *No reason. It's OK.*

And so you ask because...?

Antonio sighed. *I saw three men who looked suspicious.*

Define suspicious.

What the hell did he say to that? He had a gut feeling about them? A memory he couldn't quite pull out of the darkness of his mind even though he fumbled his way around its labyrinth during countless sleepless hours? Maybe he was going off his rocker after all. *I guess I must have made a mistake.*

You're okay, boss?

I'm fine. Thanks for asking, Gina.

You sure?

Absolutely.

You need help, you need anything at all, you let me know, va bene?

Va bene. You're one in a million, Gina. Thank you.

He put away his phone and ran his hand through his hair. Did it make sense for him to sit out here all day, in case someone came after Sofia, when Onorio's men weren't even in the area? What if Sofia stepped out of the room and found him here before he had the time to hide from her? How would she react? Maybe he ought to trust his men to warn him if there was any trouble. Maybe he should actually go home.

He stood and quietly made his way to the other end of the corridor. It was safer than walking by Nella's room again, and there had to be another way out of the hospital at that end, another lift, another staircase that led to an exit. As he came to the end and was about to turn the corner, he gasped, quickly retreating. The three shadowy figures he'd seen at the pizzeria were there, stepping out of an office with a man with round glasses in a white doctor's coat.

Antonio glued his back to the wall and held his breath as he listened.

'Make sure we have what we need by tomorrow, okay, Doc?'

'You don't seem to understand. I thought I made it clear that I can't control everything. I can't clap my hands and deliver the, hmm, stuff.'

A sarcastic laugh. Another voice. 'You have everything you need to make sure we get what we want and on time, don't you, Doc? Or like we said, we can take care of it. 'Cause we're starting to lose patience and we're not nearly as nice when our patience deserts us.'

'We'd hate for a brand new hospital like this one to meet a sad end. Things happen to hospitals, you know. They burn down, for example. I'm just saying. With all these patients in here, it'd be a real shame, right, Doc? And if that ain't enough a chief of staff could be done for dealing drugs too. I wonder how that would affect his family.'

'*Si, si,*' agreed the second man. 'No more expensive schools for the kids. No more big house, fancy cars, overseas holidays. Not even those nice leather designer shoes the wife wears. Tragic.'

Jesus, these men were Mafiosi, all right. What if they were new recruits? Or a new group that had formed recently? Maybe that was why Antonio's unit didn't know about them. What was it that they wanted from the doctor? Drugs?

'It's fine,' said the doctor, his voice trembling. 'I'll work something out. You'll have it tomorrow.'

'Good boy! He's good hey, a very clever chief of staff, this one. We'll be in touch.'

Footsteps coming in Antonio's direction signalled that the meeting was over and the men were on the move. Antonio quickly turned on his heels, only to find that the sight before him was as scary as the conversation he'd just overheard. Sofia was heading towards him like an angry bull and if there was one thing he didn't want, it was to put her in danger.

'It *is* you!' she hissed. 'I thought I was imagining things.'

He shook his head, his eyes wide with fear, and discreetly pointed behind him, hoping she'd understand that now was not the time to make a fuss, that she had to avoid at all costs attracting the attention of the men with the doctor. But how could she understand? She knew nothing of what was going on, nothing of what Antonio had been through the past month as Vice-Commander of the ROS. She had no real appreciation of the danger lurking in every corner when you were in a job like his.

If these men were part of an organised crime group, as they most probably were to tackle a hospital, and Sofia's anger made them notice her, chances were they'd see Antonio and recognise his face, too, even if today they weren't looking for him. After all, Antonio was a quasi-public figure after having appeared lately on television and at press conferences on more than one occasion, standing next to the Commander of his unit. He wasn't the star of the show—that was the Commander without a doubt—but he was still probably well-known enough to anyone from the underworld. Especially now that they were holding Onorio's brother.

Sofia's eye twitched. 'Why would you tell me you were going if—?'

Before she could finish her sentence, he grabbed her hand. 'Darling, there you are! I've been looking for you all over.' Mindful of hiding his face and Sofia's from the men on their heels, he tilted his head and pulled Sofia into the room closest to them where he firmly planted a kiss on her lips, to keep her quiet.

She shoved him away and he immediately took a step back, quickly bringing a finger to his lips to signal to her to be quiet. He expected her to scream at him, or leave shaking her head, but to his surprise and great delight she grabbed his shirt with both hands, firmly pulling him to her with need. Her lips sought his this time, nibbling them, teasing them, and she melted into Antonio, her breasts against his chest, her heart beating with his. He placed his hand on her back as he continued to taste her, kissing her softly now. She was sweet and strong at the same time, like coffee in the morning. She was warm yet as fresh as the wind of change, the only change he needed. Something in his gut told him it would take nothing more, nothing less, than Sofia herself to make him happy again.

His lips finally left hers reluctantly. 'You have no idea how glad I am that you kissed me back.'

She pressed her hand against his chest as a cheeky smile transformed her expression. 'I think I do.'

'Listen, something fishy is going on in this hospital, Sofia,' he quickly whispered. 'It's dangerous. I'm not making it up, I swear. I couldn't just go home and leave you here on your own, but I couldn't risk you being seen with me, either. The men at the restaurant? They're here, in this hospital. We have to be careful. Just give me a minute.'

He glanced through the small glass pane in the door, and then opened the door itself a crack. The men who'd threatened the doctor were nowhere to be seen. 'Looks like they're gone.'

'Who are they?'

'I'm not even sure. One thing I do know is that the less you're told, the better, Sofia. Believe me.'

'How very convenient.' She crossed her arms, her dark gaze filling suddenly with disapproval.

'I'm not having you on.' Antonio glanced at the patient in the room who was fast asleep in bed. 'At least I don't have to explain myself to that lady.'

Sofia grunted. 'I'm sure you'd come up with something far-fetched to say.'

'Look, I'm sorry I told you I was going home. This whole thing isn't ideal, I know. I'm just doing my best.'

'No, it's certainly not ideal.' She studied him for a moment, as if weighing up her options. 'At least it was a nice kiss.'

He gasped. 'Nice? That wasn't nice. That was amazing.'

Smiling, she placed a hand flat against the wall behind her and looked straight into his eyes. He let his hand come to rest next to hers, and leaned in close, so close that he could feel her warmth. He gazed at her face, at the long, dark lashes that lined her almond-shaped eyes, the perfectly plump lips that he could taste again and again if he let himself go. In the harsh hospital light most people's skin took on an unflattering colour. Not Sofia's. She was beautiful, all the time. 'I hope I'll be able to explain everything to you soon.'

'Everything?'

'Absolutely everything.' Including the past, the sleepless nights, the regrets.

'Good. You have no idea how much I'm looking forward to it.' Her expression turned serious. 'You know, if anything is going to happen between us, I need to be able to trust you.'

'I understand.' He understood perfectly. The problem was he needed to be able to protect Sofia and in his job that meant keeping things from her. He wasn't sure how to reconcile the two. 'How is Nella?' he asked, dragging himself to safer ground.

'She's much better, thanks. She seems so much brighter all of a sudden; she has all this renewed energy. She sat up and ate a full meal an hour ago. She's been so chatty. It's just like before. I mean, like months ago. I was really surprised and I don't have to tell you how pleased I am.'

'That's fabulous news.' He was thrilled for Nella, for Sofia, for himself too. He'd always adored Nella.

'Maybe she'll be out of here soon,' ventured Sofia.

'I sincerely hope so. It would be lovely.'

'Thank you.' As she smiled at him, he inched a little closer to her, once again drawn to her like an insect to a lamp in the middle of the night. She was his light, his one and only source of light, he had no doubt about that.

She linked her fingers with his and butterflies fluttered about his stomach at the unexpected touch of her soft skin. Would she let him kiss her again if he tried, now that they'd cleared the air? Now that they were okay?

He inched closer still and was about to bend his head, desire already burning through his body, when a cry of agony pierced the air.

Fear flashed through Sofia's eyes. 'Zia Nella!' She dashed into the corridor and then her aunt's room while Antonio hurried in behind her, through the door that swung back and forth with the force of Sofia's worry.

Nella sat on the bed, a harrowed expression on her face, and picked at the sheets, pulling, twisting and turning them relentlessly.

'*Zia*, what is it? What's wrong?'

'No! It's coming for me. Grab it! Hit it! Hurry! Can't you see its teeth? Ah!' Nella covered her head with her arms, protecting herself from an invisible enemy. 'Help! They're so sharp! It hurts so much.' She let out a wail.

Antonio placed a hand on Sofia's trembling shoulder. 'She's delirious. I'll call the nurse.' He pressed the red button next to Nella's bed.

'But she was better.' The confusion in Sofia's eyes broke Antonio's heart. If there was anything he could do to take away her pain, he would.

'Monster!' Nella threw her pillows across the room. 'Get it! There! It's going to bite us.'

'Stop, *zia!* There's nothing here. It must be the medication.' Sofia wrapped her arms around Nella. 'You're seeing things. There's no monster.'

'No!' Nella brutally pushed her niece away and started pulling savagely at her own hair, a white tuft coming away in her hand.

'God, where's the nurse?' Sofia's voice caught in her throat.

Antonio pressed the button again. 'Do you want to go and get someone? I'll stay here.'

'Oh, look!' cried Nella. 'Look! It's Grandma Angela! Sofia, it's my *nonna*.' Nella laughed, an expression of wonder on her face for a second. 'I'm going to be with her soon.'

'There's no one here, *zia*.'

'I'm telling you, she's here. You don't believe me, huh? Traitors. All traitors.' Nella bitterly spat on the floor before turning to pummel the bed.

Sofia let out her breath. 'I can't leave her. You fetch someone.'

'Be careful while I'm gone. I'll be quick.' Antonio rushed out the door and down the corridor to the nurse's station. 'Help!' he cried. There was only one nurse behind the desk, on the phone. He talked over her conversation, his voice loud and clear. 'We need help. The patient's delirious and very agitated, lashing out. Room 213.'

'I have to go.' The woman hung up, grabbed a box out of a cupboard and came running behind Antonio to Nella's room, pressing on a beeper. A security officer soon appeared and followed them.

When they got there, Sofia was holding Nella down on the bed and the floor was littered with glass, most likely a smashed vase. 'Quick,' she said, tears streaming down her cheeks. 'I can't keep her still much longer. She's stronger than she looks.'

Antonio and the security guard took over, holding down Nella while the nurse injected something into her arm. 'This is Haldol,' she explained. 'It will calm her down almost immediately.' She nodded her thanks to Antonio and the guard, who let go of Nella. 'The doctor will be here any minute.'

Sofia wiped her tears with the back of her hand. 'Thank you.' Antonio swallowed hard, hoping the lump that had formed in his throat at the sight of Sofia's pain and stopped him from speaking, would loosen.

Nella's arms quickly went limp and she closed her eyes, falling into a deep sleep.

'Are you all right, dear?' asked the nurse patting Sofia's arm.

Sofia nodded. 'I will be. Thanks. It's so hard to see my aunt like this.'

'Of course. She'll sleep now for a while. I'll send someone to clean up the glass.'

The nurse left and Antonio wrapped his arms around Sofia, drawing her to him. 'I'm so sorry.' The sight of Nella picking, scratching, screaming had been horrible and he wished he could wipe the image from Sofia's memory.

'I've never seen her like that,' whispered Sofia. 'I've never seen anything like that. I don't understand.'

'Neither do I.'

There was a knock at the door and Sofia pulled away as a young doctor entered. 'Hello,

I'm Doctor Pagnani. The nurse has filled me in on what happened. It would seem that Mrs Conti has suffered an episode of psychotic behaviour. It isn't uncommon for people in your aunt's condition.'

Sofia blinked repeatedly. 'The thing is, she was better. She had a full meal for the first time in ages. She was bright. I was thinking she'd be coming home, maybe even today, that this hospital stay had been a false alert. That it wasn't...' Sofia placed her hand over her mouth, unable to finish her sentence.

'Let's step out of the room for a moment,' said the doctor, gesturing to the door. 'In fact, let's go and sit down.' Sofia and Antonio followed him out and he led them to a waiting area, a sitting room with plastic coffee tables, a collection of magazines and grey upholstered chairs where they made themselves comfortable.

'Would you like some water?' The doctor gestured to a water dispenser in the corner.

'I'm fine, thanks,' said Sofia while Antonio simply shook his head.

'I'd rather not speak in front of the patient as we suspect some are able to hear what is going on around them, even after sedation.'

'Right,' said Antonio.

'We have the results of the tests we ran on Mrs Conti earlier, and I'm afraid that the news isn't good. You ought to make sure her affairs are in order.'

'No, no.' Sofia moved back in her seat. 'I do understand what you're saying ... but not with *zia* Nella. There's been a mistake. She got better today. She ate a full meal for the first time in ages. She was bright, sprightly and...' Her bottom lip quivered.

Antonio ran his hand up Sofia's arm. Why couldn't he take away her pain? Why couldn't he spare her what was about to come?

'I'm sorry,' continued the doctor. 'I understand that it can be a distressing time for family members, but it is often the case that patients show great improvement for a short time.'

Sofia made a fist with her hand. 'She's going to be okay now. She's sleeping, that's all. She had an outburst, sure, but she's not going to be like that again.'

'The medication we have administered will keep her calm for as long as possible. That said, we can't rule out similar episodes again.'

'You're saying this is going to be a regular occurrence?' Sofia turned to Antonio with eyes full of sorrow and a knot formed in his stomach. 'How often?'

'No, not a regular occurrence as such. This usually indicates...' He took a deep breath. 'It usually occurs as the process commences.'

Antonio frowned. 'The *process?*'

The doctor cleared his throat. 'The dying process. We now know that a gradual shutdown of the body occurs in an organised way. The delirium, the agitation you just witnessed are often part of that process and can reoccur as it progresses. We are lucky that the medication has worked for her on this occasion.'

Tears rolled down Sofia's cheeks and she dropped her gaze to the floor. 'It was just awful. Does it have to be like this?'

Antonio wrapped his arms around her.

'We do our best to give the patients all the relief we can,' mumbled Pagnani.

'How long does she have, Doctor?' asked Sofia.

'It's impossible to say for sure, but it's close. I'd say a day or two.' The young doctor pursed his lips. 'I'm sorry.'

Sofia gasped for air. Antonio pulled her closer and ran his hand over her hair.

'You ought to rest for a while, take some time to recover,' said Doctor Pagnani. 'And contact me if you need anything.'

Antonio watched the young doctor carefully. Something told him that everyone in this hospital should be treated with suspicion. Were there any signs Pagnani was nervous? Any signs he was lying? Not that he could see. Antonio nodded to let the young man know they'd be all right and the doctor disappeared down the corridor, the sound of his hurried steps fading quickly.

Alone again with Antonio, Sofia finally let go of all restraint. She shuddered, her slight frame wracked by sobs while Antonio held her. When she let out the bellow of a wounded animal, he kissed her forehead fighting back his own tears that threatened to spill at the sight of her agony.

He'd give anything to help her, anything to take away the ache in her, the shock, the loss. He'd trade years of his life for Sofia not to have to go through this earthquake today.

But there was nothing he could offer to wash away her pain.

All he could do was be there.

Chapter 9

Sofia watched her aunt sleep in peace. Would she be dead two days from now? Would she wake only to live another nightmare of imaginary monsters and visions of ghosts and try to tear out her own hair? Sofia hoped with all her heart that the doctor was wrong on both accounts. Thank goodness Antonio had been here to help. Even now that he had stepped into the corridor to make a few work phone calls, it was reassuring to know that he was seconds away.

Rushed footsteps reached her door and yet another doctor Sofia hadn't seen before entered, a man of a certain age with round glasses and a somewhat dorky face. He looked the way she imagined Harry Potter would in middle age.

'*Buongiorno.* I'm chief of staff, Doctor Rinotto. I'm taking over from Doctor Pagnani in Mrs, euh...' He checked the name on the file he was carrying. 'Mrs Conti's case.'

'You're her doctor now?' Why the abrupt change? If Nella really only had a day or two to live, why bother to get a different person involved? And a chief of staff too. Unless there was a problem—an unexpected test result, a mix-up, a misdiagnosis. 'Is something the matter?'

Doctor Pagnani's diagnosis was wrong. She's not dying. Please let it be that.

'Let me reassure you, nothing's the matter. Doctor Pagnani has a number of complex cases and can no longer attend to all of his previous patients. Don't worry, your, hmm...'

'My aunt.'

'Yes, your aunt, is in good hands.'

The chief of staff felt Nella's pulse, lifted up her left eyelid.

'So she's all right?' Stress stiffened Sofia's shoulders.

The doctor nodded. 'Absolutely. This is routine. You needn't worry.'

Sofia crossed her arms. Something about this man bothered her, something she couldn't quite put her finger on. Perhaps it was the way he avoided her gaze. But she had to know. She steeled herself. 'Excuse me, but the previous doctor said my aunt only had a few days to live. He talked about the *dying process*. The thing is, *zia* Nella was very bright just before this all started. She ate a full meal. I hadn't seen her like that for such a long time. There was real improvement, and then this ... this episode of *madness*. Do you think it could be something else, a mental issue? Something temporary?' Something that could be fixed with a pill or two, and Nella would be sent home? Sofia hoped so with all her heart. 'Could it be that Doctor Pagnani has perhaps misdiagnosed her?'

'It can be very distressing for family members but it isn't unusual for there to be a sudden improvement just before a further deterioration.'

'I'm not sure I understand. Are you saying you agree with what the previous doctor said?'

'I have every confidence in Doctor Pagnani. I have read your aunt's file and discussed matters with him, and I am sorry to say that we are in complete agreement.'

The floor seemed to move under her feet. Sofia held onto the back of a chair as she blinked back tears. One doctor could be wrong, but two? And a chief of staff was someone with considerable experience, wasn't it? She opened her mouth, the sudden pain shooting through her making her gasp.

Rinotto took a syringe out of a pouch.

'What is that?' asked Sofia through laboured breaths. Nella was sleeping like a baby and had been injected with strong drugs less than half an hour ago. Why did she need another shot?

'It's ... something to help her rest.' The doctor's eye twitched.

'What do you mean? She's already resting.' Sofia looked down at the chief of staff's hand. It was trembling. She examined his face. How pale he was! He put down the needle, wiped his forehead, and picked the needle up again, holding it above Nella's arm.

Why was he waiting? Hesitating?

'Antonio!' screamed Sofia, giving in to the sudden urge to have him by her side, right here, right now.

Within seconds Antonio came rushing in, throwing open the door as if the place was on fire. 'Are you okay?'

'Antonio, another doctor's here,' answered Sofia. 'Doctor Rinotto, the—'

'Chief of staff,' said Antonio, finishing her sentence and stepping forward until he stood in the doctor's face. 'Put that down.'

Needle in hand, the doctor stared at the Vice-Commander of the ROS. 'And who are you to tell me how to look after my patients?' He blinked. 'You look familiar, actually.' The doctor took a laboured breath.

'I get that a lot. I'm Antonio De Santis. I work with Commander Carone who is often on television, with me by his side.'

If looks could kill, Antonio would have shot the doctor dead there and then, his grey-green gaze as cold as the bullets that filled his gun. Did he have a gun with him? Sofia wondered.

Rinotto grunted. 'Yes, of course. I knew I'd seen you somewhere.' He quickly put the syringe back in the pouch he'd carried it in, gesturing towards Nella. 'I was just checking she didn't need more sedatives. She's fine for now. Someone will call in to see her later,' he mumbled before hurrying out.

Antonio frowned and reached for Sofia, taking her hands in his.

Gazing into his eyes she let out her breath. It was such a relief to have him in the room with her again, such sweet comfort knowing that he would protect her and Nella. 'I'm sorry I screamed like that. I just had a bad feeling about that doctor and I ... I didn't know what else to do.' She'd needed Antonio, as much as she needed the air in her lungs.

'Wait here.' Nino dashed towards the door.

'Antonio? Where are you going?'

'I need to talk to that guy. Anything happens, anyone turns up unexpectedly, you phone me straight away, okay? Even if it's just a gut feeling. You have good instincts, you know that?'

She smiled. 'I will. I'll call straight away. Thank you, Antonio.'

'For what?' He opened his hands as if to say that he hadn't done anything.

'For being by my side through all this. It isn't easy, and I really appreciate it.'

'It's the least I can do. Besides, I always knew we'd make a good team.' The sincerity in his grey-green eyes set off butterflies in her stomach. If she let herself go, if she ignored reason and followed her need, she'd allow herself to drown in that gaze forever, the way she wanted to before she'd even turned sixteen. She'd grab him right there and then, hold onto him and never let him go.

He moved to the door, stopping in front of it and turned around. 'I forgot something.' With three giant steps he was back by Sofia's side. He placed his hands on her back, drew her to him, and his lips found hers. The softness of his skin, the sweetness of his breath, made her head spin and her heart pound her chest, and she hung onto him for fear that her legs wouldn't hold her up.

When she kissed him back, groaning with pleasure, he held her tighter and ignited the fire in her with the passion of the young man she once knew. It was as if the world had suddenly stopped spinning around, as if nothing else existed, only Antonio, and she had become every image of him she'd ever seen, every word she'd heard him say, every scent, every sensation that had come from him. She was his hand in her hair as they'd stood together in the shade of the church, his smile as they'd counted the stars in the sky, his green-grey gaze meeting hers as he'd climbed off his Vespa. She was the knowing look they'd exchanged at the bakery, her wet feet when she'd crossed the flooded road to see him, his fingers brushing against hers as he'd handed her the gelato he'd bought for her. And now she was his arms cradling her when she'd hurt her ankle, his gift of flowers and cakes, his lips on hers in the hospital, and everything they'd lived since they'd met again as adults.

Sofia's past had found the present, all in a kiss.

***

Antonio marched down the corridor in search of Chief of Staff Rinotto, the same guy he'd seen with the men from the pizzeria, those who'd threatened to burn down the hospital if he didn't deliver the goods, whatever they might be, the next day.

What had the man been doing at Nella's bedside, with an injection of so-called sedatives that Nella clearly didn't need as she was fast asleep? The conversation he'd overheard in the corridor came back to him.

I can't clap my hands and deliver the, hmm, stuff.

You have everything you need to make sure we get what we want and on time, don't you, Doc?

What if the goods weren't drugs? What if it was body parts they were trafficking? Antonio shivered at the thought, at what that had nearly meant for Nella if he was right. If Sofia hadn't screamed for him, if the chief of staff hadn't recognised Antonio as someone from the *carabinieri,* would the physician have gone through with it?

As he turned the corner he saw Rinotto at the nurses' station, thankfully leaning over the desk with his back to Antonio so he wouldn't see him coming. Otherwise, he suspected, Rinotto might make a run for it, making an excuse not to have to speak to the man who represented the law.

Antonio quietly walked up to the chief of staff and placed his hand on the man's shoulder. Rinotto jumped.

'It's only me, Doctor, Antonio De Santis. I'd like to have a word in private.'

'Hmm, I'm run off my feet right now.' Rather, he seemed frozen on his feet.

'*Please,*' he insisted. Tempted to stick his gun in the guy's back, Antonio simply raised an eyebrow. 'It's very important.'

'Follow me.' Nearly as pale as the white coat he wore, Rinotto led the way to his office a few steps down the corridor, a simple white room with a beige melamine desk and matching metal filing cabinets.

He gestured for Antonio to sit on one of the grey padded visitor chairs. 'What can I do for you?' he asked from behind his desk, a bead of sweat forming on his brow.

'To start with, you can tell me what you were about to inject into Mrs Conti that would have no doubt led to her death.'

'How dare you come in here and accuse me of unspeakable things!' The chief of staff pointed to the door, his hand shaking. 'Leave now before I call security.'

'I heard those men talking to you in the corridor. I heard their threats. I know how the Mafia works. You're not acting of your own free will. You're under duress. We can protect you and your family, but you have to tell us everything.'

Rinotto's whole frame shuddered and he covered his eyes with his hands. The tears he shed silently ran along his neck, landing on the papers in front of him on his desk. 'I didn't know where to go for help,' he managed to whisper through his sobs. 'I couldn't live without my wife or my daughter. I'm so, so scared for them.'

'We'll make sure you and your family are safe.' Antonio knew from experience that it was possible, even if it would come at a non-negligible personal cost. It would mean a break in Rinotto's career, a house move, a country move if necessary, leaving behind pretty much everyone he'd ever met and every place he'd ever loved.

'Okay.' The distressed man wiped his face on his sleeve.

'Did you inject anything into Nella?'

'Nella?'

'Mrs Conti.'

'Oh. No, not just then.'

Antonio's jaw tightened. 'Before?'

'I, hmm, yes, before her visions. I slipped into her room at one stage. But she'll be all right. I only injected a trace amount. I couldn't do more than that. I couldn't go through with it. And then they threatened me again and ... You have to understand, I had to.' He hid his eyes with his hand. 'I thought I'd pick an elderly patient since there's no age limit on organ donation, that way, I was robbing them of less years.'

Antonio huffed. 'Organ *donation*? Is that what you call it?' He shook his head. 'Tell me, is Doctor Pagnani involved, or anyone else?'

The chief of staff shook his head. 'No, Pagnani isn't, not knowingly. No one is. Just me.'

'Not knowingly?'

'I swapped over some medication he's given Mrs Conti, and some test results, but he had no way of figuring that out.'

'But Pagnani was the one who talked about her entering the dying process. I thought he'd invented that, to explain what was about to happen to Nella.'

'No. That was his diagnosis, and it is something that we do see in hospitals, believe me. It's starting to be more widely recognised medically that the body goes through a shutdown process, very often accompanied by hallucinations where people see those who have gone before them. And they get very angry if you don't believe them. But in Mrs Conti's case the medication was responsible for the visions.'

'When it was pre-meditated murder that was on the cards.' Antonio tapped the desk, while he would have loved for his fist to connect with the doctor's jaw as payback for what he'd put Nella through, what he'd put Sofia through even if he knew the chief of staff hadn't been acting of his own free will. 'Can you confirm it's the Mafia that has been visiting you?'

'I'm sure it is, or *Cosa Nostra*, whatever they call themselves, although no one has told me so. I'm aware it's organised crime.'

'*Cosa Nostra*'s the Sicilian mob. It could be the *Camorra*, from Naples which isn't that far from here, the *Ndrangheta* from Calabria, also not too far, or a number of other organisations trying to set up shop in the region. They didn't refer to a particular group?'

'No. I said *Cosa Nostra* because it was the first name that came to mind.'

Cosa Nostra. Our business. Antonio shook his head. It was his business, too, his business to stop them. 'How are you aware it's organised crime? I mean, what makes you say that?'

'There's a group of them involved.'

'How many?'

'I see three men, but I've heard them mention others. And there's a hierarchy. They talk about the boss and the big boss.'

'And what do they want, the guys who are after you?'

'A heart and two kidneys by tomorrow afternoon, as well as the *pizzo*, regular payments for their so-called *protection*.'

'They're coming here for the organs?'

'No. There's a drop-off in town. They've organised a fake ambulance. It will wait for me at the east end of via Falcone.'

'Tell me something. Has this happened before? An organ drop-off?'

The doctor shook his head. 'We haven't been open that long. And the first few weeks all they wanted was drugs.'

Antonio let out his breath. At least no one had been killed so far. It had nearly been Nella's heart and two kidneys, though. He knew how the Mafia could weigh on its 'collaborators', encouraging them to participate in organised crime through threats and cruel lessons, using families and friends as examples. They could make even strong, righteous people bend to their ways. It hurt to find out that one of his own had come this close to death, because Nella and Sofia were his own. He cared about them. It didn't matter that Nella was old and ill. She deserved to be here for the rest of her natural life, deserved not to be robbed of even a minute of it, and it wouldn't be fair for Sofia to lose her aunt before her time, either.

That was the very best reason to catch these bastards, to lock them up and throw away the key. There were phone calls to make, and a lot to put in place, an awful lot to think about, but Antonio had a plan. 'Okay then.' He walked over and placed a hand on the doctor's shoulder. 'I want you to know that if you cooperate fully it's going to be fine. Everything's going to be just fine. We'll protect you.'

'It's not me I'm worried about.'

'We'll keep you and your family safe, and anyone who's close to you who might be at risk.'

'OK. I'll do anything you want.'

'Good. Here's what I need you to do.'

***

Sitting in the corner of the room, Sofia ran her fingers over her lips. Even though nearly two hours had gone by since Antonio had taken her in his arms, she could still feel his kiss and the fire in him that had burned through her entire body.

It was so good. He was so good.

How long had it been since she'd felt that comfortable and warm in someone's arms? Certainly a while. The two years spent with Terry had been a succession of moments of fear, disgust and despair.

If only this thing that was developing between Antonio and her were happening at a better time. If only Nella were well. She looked at her aunt, the lines on her kind face, the silver hair, the sun spots on the skin of her hands, and the word that came to mind wasn't old or sick. It was *beloved*. Sofia loved her with all her imperfections and maybe she felt the true weight of her affection now that Nella had seemingly little time left.

Sofia took a deep breath and wished for an easy end for her aunt. She sighed. The end was probably never easy. It was a stupid comparison, but she thought of the pets she'd had over the years. How many of those had died quietly in their sleep? Not one. The end had always been a struggle for them and she suspected it would have been even more so without euthanasia. Why would it be any different for humans?

Nella stirred, drawing Sofia out of her thoughts. The old woman opened her eyes, her gaze darting around aimlessly.

'*Zia!* I'm here!' Sofia jumped up and rushed to her side, trying to ignore the niggling worry that tightened her muscles. What if Nella was still seeing monsters? What if she lashed out again at her?

'Sofia, my love. How long have I been asleep? It feels like it must be a hundred years, like the princess in *Sleeping Beauty.*' She looked at the clock on the bedside cabinet. 'Oh! I've had a good few hours.'

'It's *you, zia* Nella!' Tears welled in Sofia's eyes. 'You're back.'

'What on earth do you mean? Of course it's me.'

'You're awake and you're back to your normal self.' Sofia hugged the frail old woman with enthusiasm, lifting her off the pillow. 'I knew it. I knew it would be all right. I love you, *zia.*'

'I love you too, sweetheart. What happened? Did I do something strange?'

'You don't remember?' She gently placed her aunt back down. 'You had visions of monsters. You were very agitated. You gave me the fright of my life.'

'I was seeing things? I'm sorry if I scared you.'

Sofia grinned. 'It's okay, it's over now. That's all that matters.'

'You're on your own?' Nella glanced around the room.

'Antonio's been here. He's attending to some business now.' He'd been kind enough to send her a message and let her know that after speaking to the chief of staff he had some work to do. 'He's been gone for nearly two hours. He helped a lot while you, hmm, had that episode.'

'He's a good lad, that one, Sofia.' Nella waved her finger at her niece, marking her words.

Sofia smiled. She wasn't about to admit to her aunt that she agreed. But she did agree now, with all her heart. And her head was starting to think that way too. Perhaps not all men were controlling bastards after all. Perhaps there really were exceptions to the rule and Antonio was one of them—she was beginning to see just how brilliant an exception if ever there was one. Actually, perhaps the controlling bastards were the exceptions after all and there were a lot of good ones out there. She smiled. It was a nice thought.

The door to the room swung open and Antonio entered. 'Speaking of the devil,' said Sofia with a smile because in fact she was starting to see him as an angel.

'That's not the right expression for this lovely young man,' replied Nella.

Antonio chuckled. 'Not that young. Not that lovely, either, if I'm being realistic.'

'Oh, Antonio, don't be too hard on yourself,' said Sofia, glancing at him.

His smile was so warm that it melted her heart. 'I'm happy you feel that way, Sofia.' He turned back to Nella. 'Good to see you're awake and chatty, Nella. Really good. How are you feeling?'

'Never better. Not for ages, anyway.'

'That's great.' He looked over at Sofia. 'Everything all right?'

She nodded. It was all she could do while his grey-green eyes sent a shiver down her spine, a shiver of delight at the attention he was giving her and the memory of the kiss they'd shared earlier. She ached to step closer to him, to lean against him, but she couldn't. It was too soon to behave like lovers, especially in front of Nella. 'Have you sorted out all your work?'

'I have. It's all under control. By the way, you won't be seeing any more of the chief of staff. He's going to be off the hospital grounds for a while.'

Sofia's eyes widened. 'But I thought he was replacing Doctor Pagnani. Does that mean we are getting yet another doctor now?'

'No, Doctor Pagnani will be looking after Nella again. They're going to run some new tests to see why you were bleeding at home, Nella. They'll come and talk to you about it. I told them they'd better do everything by the book with you or they'll have to deal with me. And I'm not the easiest man to deal with.'

The bright patient chuckled. 'Thank you, Antonio.'

Sofia smiled at him, hoping he could see the gratitude in her eyes.

I would have been lost without you through all this.

She would tell him so. Maybe not now, not here, not just yet.

But soon.

Very soon.

She'd tell him that he'd mattered to her since the day he'd parked his Vespa just to pick a tiny wild orchid on the side of the road and offer it to her. The memory warmed her heart. Yes, Antonio had mattered to her for a very long time, that was patently clear to her now.

He'd mattered more than any man ever had and that she was so glad he was in her life.

Chapter 10

Antonio kept a close eye on Sofia as Doctor Pagnani gestured for them to take a seat on the visitor chairs in her aunt's hospital room. Her whole being tensed with anxiety, more so than poor Nella who seemed resigned to whatever medical news the young man brought. Antonio placed his hand on Sofia's forearm, half-expecting her to move away. She didn't. She accepted his comfort even in front of her old aunt, and that filled Antonio's heart with a joy he didn't dare talk about for fear that it would change.

'Good morning,' said Doctor Pagnani with the utmost seriousness.

'Good morning,' came the joint reply of Sofia, Nella and Antonio.

'The gastroenterologist you saw, Doctor Nobusso, isn't available as he's in surgery, so I'm here to go over his findings with you. Would you like everyone to step out while I do that?' the young doctor asked Nella.

The patient shook her head. 'Anything you say to me, you can say in front of these two.'

'I'm cautiously pleased,' said Pagnani, a smile suddenly illuminating his face, 'and I think you will be, too, with the report of the gastroenterologist. I say cautiously because he recommends his findings be confirmed by a sigmoidoscopy, but he is quite confident that the bleeding you experienced was a haemorrhoidal occurrence. On rare occasions, haemorrhoids result in severe blood loss.'

He held out a page that Nella took. She slipped on her glasses and glanced over it. After a moment, she burst into laughter while tears of joy rolled down her cheeks. 'I'm sorry, I just thought it was the leukaemia ... Haemorrhoids! If I've survived leukaemia I should survive haemorrhoids for a while.'

Sofia let out her breath and grinned at Antonio. 'That's great news!'

Antonio nodded, relief washing over him for Nella, for Sofia. He returned her smile. 'It certainly is fabulous news.'

Pagnani's lips curled up as he watched their joyful reactions. 'I think we all agree on that. You may, however, require a small operation, depending on how it presents.'

'So the test to confirm, when do I do that?' asked Nella as she finally stopped giggling.

'Tomorrow, late afternoon. We'll put you on a diet of liquids until then. You needn't worry about it, it's a ten-minute exam and we'll keep you comfortable right through it.'

Nella shrugged. 'Doctor, when you've been thinking you're about to check out the next day, and I don't mean out of hospital, I mean the final departure, a ten-minute exam isn't something you worry about too much.'

Sofia moved closer to her aunt and patted the old woman's hand. 'You watch, you'll be home before you know it.'

The doctor left a leaflet about the next day's sigmoidoscopy before leaving.

'I might be discharged this time tomorrow,' said Nella softly.

'I told you it wasn't the last time you'd see your home,' said Antonio.

'You did too.' Nella lay back down, beaming. 'I'm so happy my cheeks are hurting. The ones on my face, not my bottom, although I do admit to having been a pain in the arse.'

They all shared a laugh at Nella's joke. 'I'm rather tired as well, having said that,' she continued. 'You two should go home, get something to eat. I could do with some rest and I'm sure you'd appreciate a break from this drab place.'

Antonio's gaze met Sofia's. Should he invite her to dinner? He was dying to. But what would she say? Was she ready for that? 'I suppose we should get a bite and call it a day, especially as tomorrow could be hectic.'

Sofia frowned. 'Hectic?'

168

'Oh, I haven't mentioned that? More work stuff. I'm sorry.'

'No problem. Work for you, tests for Nella. Well, I'm planning on a lovely, relaxing morning without either of you.'

Antonio let out a laugh. 'If I didn't know better I'd think you were happy about getting rid of me. Of the two of us, hey, Nella?'

Nella chuckled. 'That's my Sofia.'

Antonio tapped the old woman's shoulder. 'You have a good rest. I'll see you tomorrow.'

He watched as Sofia closed her eyes and pressed her lips to Nella's forehead, to say goodbye to her dear aunt. Beneath her tough exterior, Sofia was all softness and love. A kind heart, a determined, cheeky mind, the face of an angel and a body that ... he couldn't think too hard about that body or he'd be walking funny. Ah, gorgeous Sofia! There wasn't a better mix.

They strolled side-by-side to the lift. 'Such good news about Nella,' he said softly.

'You can say that again.'

'Such good news about Nella.'

She grinned. 'That's what kids do, repeat the sentence they've just said when you say, *you can say that again.*'

'Maybe that's because you make me feel like a kid again.' She did. She made him feel like the enthusiastic, happy teen full of hope that he used to be. The kid who was in love with Sofia.

The door to the lift opened and they stepped inside. Her perfume filled his lungs with sweetness and his head with dreams. 'Have dinner with me tonight, Sofia.'

She dropped her gaze to the floor before looking straight into his eyes, setting fire to his belly. He hung onto the metal rail in the lift so as not to grab her with both hands, pull her to him, lift up her leg and ... God, just one look at her and it drove him crazy, had him imagining her body naked and more than that, an intimacy he so needed to share with her.

'I'd like that,' she whispered.

He let out a sharp breath. Yes! She'd said yes. 'My house at eight? I'll cook for you.'

She blinked twice. 'Your house?'

'Why not? It'll be nicer. We can just sit and chat in peace and not have to worry about the people around us. If it's too much, we can go to a restaurant but ... I promise you it will be dinner and that's all, if that's what you want it to be. No pressure whatsoever.' He wanted nothing more than to feel her skin against his, but he was a man of his word and whatever suited Sofia would suit him.

They stepped out of the lift and headed past the gift shop to the main entrance.

She rubbed her nose. 'Sounds great. Your house. Shall I bring dessert?'

'That's out of the question in Italy. You don't bring a thing, except perhaps a bottle of wine or flowers for the lady of the house, but I have enough alcohol in my cellar for an army and I don't like to think of myself as the lady of the house.'

She giggled, her infectious laughter making him chuckle too, although he was so happy he could have laughed on his own like a madman for no reason whatsoever.

As they stepped out of the hospital grounds, he corrected himself in his mind. Even if he laughed on his own, it wouldn't be for no reason. He was going home to cook for the magnificent woman he'd wanted in his life since he was seventeen and that was the best reason in the world to be happy.

***

Sofia parked in front of Nino's double-storey house, a vine-covered flat-roofed home with French doors opening onto the garden, and climbed out of her aunt Nella's ancient Fiat Panda. It was strange to be driving around all dressed up in an old bomb. She straightened her black chiffon dress, hoping she hadn't gone overboard. It was perhaps a bit much, but she only had one going-out dress, hadn't brought anything else suitable for a date, and jeans and a shirt didn't feel right tonight.

A date. My goodness, that's what this is. With Nino De Santis. How long since I went on a date?

She swallowed hard and then she shook herself as she walked through his wrought iron gate to his front door. It could just be dinner with a friend, if that's what she wanted. He'd made that clear. What did she want? Did she even know for sure?

What she did know was that her heart was pounding in her chest as she was about to knock, but before her fist made contact with the shiny wood, the door opened. Nino must have heard her park.

'Hello, Sofia. Perfect timing.' His gaze wandered down her body before settling on her face again. 'You look magnificent. I, uh...' He pointed to his shirt. 'I'm sorry, I'm a bit under-dressed. You'll have to forgive me.'

She smiled. He looked perfect to her in his grey linen shirt and fawn pants. 'You look just fine. I didn't have anything else to wear to dinner. I packed light when I came over. I don't like carting around heavy suitcases.'

He welcomed her in with a warm gesture. The house was charming with its stone floors and eclectic furniture, a variety of styles that somehow worked perfectly together. 'I love your home. It's beautiful.'

'Thank you. I love it too, except it's not mine. It belongs to a friend of my mother's.'

'It's the mix that works.'

'I'll show you around later, if you like.'

'That would be lovely.' Seeing his house would have been better, though. It would have made her feel closer to him, as if she'd finally been allowed into his intimacy after all these years. Maybe one day, maybe soon. 'Do your mum and dad come here often these days?'

'Hmm, no. Not anymore. They, well, they don't come here now.'

'You see them in Rome?'

'No.' He paused, averting his gaze. 'They used to visit me a lot.'

Sofia wondered why his lips twisted with unease. Had they fought? Were they no longer in touch? She thought it better not to dig too deep about it right now. Whatever it was, he obviously wasn't ready to talk about it. He didn't have to tell her absolutely everything straight away for her to trust him, did he?

Just because he wasn't comfortable sharing something didn't mean he was hiding important things from her, did it?

She brushed the niggling doubt away. Not everyone was like her ex-husband. It was time to trust a man again and it didn't mean he had to disclose every single fact about himself immediately. It would be unreasonable of her to think that way. People nearly always needed time to reveal themselves and their stories to others. Perhaps it was those who didn't wait, those who blurted out every secret they'd ever had, that were to be watched.

Nino led her to the dining room where he'd set the table with exquisite china and a small bouquet of flowers from the garden. It was so sweet of him that her heart melted at the effort he'd made. 'What a beautiful table.'

He smiled, gesturing for her to take a seat. 'Would you like something to drink first? Martini, Chinotto, Campari? Or fruit juice?'

'A Campari would be lovely.'

He disappeared into the kitchen for a moment and returned with the ruby red aperitif in two sparkling glasses topped with a slice of orange.

Sofia took a sip and let the alcohol work its way through her body, relaxing her shoulders. She let out a long breath.

That's better. There's nothing to be nervous about.

A delicious scent of cooking wafted through the air. 'I can smell dinner.'

'I must have left the kitchen door open when I got the Campari. I'll go and close it.'

'Please don't. It smells delicious. Am I allowed to ask what it is?'

'Osso buco. I hope you like it.'

'I'm a vegetarian.'

'Oh, *Dio mio!* I should have asked. I can make you a salad.'

She burst into laughter. 'I'm kidding. I don't eat meat very often, but I do have it sometimes.'

He leaned back in his chair, pressing his hand to his heart. 'You nearly gave me a heart attack.'

'I'm sorry. Just a little joke.'

He gave her a cheeky glance, one that sent a tingle of anticipation down her spine. 'You're naughty, Sofia. I'll make you pay for that one day.'

Her lips curled into a smile. 'I'll be waiting.' She took another sip of her aperitif. The banter was easy, enjoyable, enticing. Being here on her own, at a pretty table with the gorgeous man that was Nino, made her feel all woman again.

'Oh, I forgot the nibbles.' Antonio jumped up, returning almost instantly with a plate of dried sausage, prosciutto, olives, artichokes and cherry tomatoes. He pointed to the vegetables. 'Something for the vegetarian here.'

Sofia giggled and helped herself to a few olives and tomatoes. 'Thanks. It's so nice of you to have done all this. You cook often?'

He nodded. 'I love to cook. It relaxes me. When I'm chopping onions, I forget all my work troubles. That's probably because I'm too busy wiping my tears.'

'Ah, I have that problem with onions too.' She chuckled again. 'I can just imagine you balling your eyes out above a chopping board. At least we didn't end up crying over Nella's fate tonight.'

'No, and I'm so happy about that. I bet you are too.'

She nodded. The evening could have taken a drastically different turn. She raised her glass. 'To the way the day turned out.'

He clinked his glass to hers. 'To good times ahead.'

She swallowed another mouthful of the bright red drink, watching him while he did the same. Was it the way he looked at her above his glass, his grey-green eyes sending a shiver of excitement through her body? Or how he licked his lips, savouring the Campari and reminding her of the kisses they'd shared at the hospital? She wasn't sure. All she knew was that she had to feel him against her again. Right now.

She put down her glass, went over to him and took his glass, placing it on the table. She cupped his face, that gorgeous, strong, square jaw of his fitting perfectly in her hands, and bent down, her lips seeking his. She kissed him the way she'd wanted to when they were young, with everything in her, if only she'd felt that he'd gotten to know her first. But the past didn't matter now. The only thing that mattered was that they had another chance, a better chance this time, and she was going to make the most of it.

Her whole body tingled with pleasure and when he stood and took her in his arms, kissing her back with more passion than she'd ever thought possible, her legs trembled and weakened. He must have felt her shakiness, must have feared she'd fall, for he held her tighter, wrapping both arms around her waist and almost lifting her off the floor.

It was as if her body melted into his, as if they became one at that moment, and everything around them ceased to exist. Life was his kiss, his embrace and nothing else. Life was pleasure and warmth and heart. Life was Nino.

When they finally came up for air, he rubbed his nose against hers. 'I wasn't expecting that,' he whispered. 'At least not so soon.'

'To tell you the truth, nor was I.' She hadn't planned it. It had just happened. She'd had the urge to do it and she'd followed her gut. And now, she was swimming in happiness.

He grinned. 'I love the unexpected.' His face suddenly transformed, his brow creasing, his jaw tightening, his expression hardening so much that he barely resembled the Antonio she knew. It reminded her of the metamorphosis Terry could undergo in the blink of an eye, from Prince Charming to the deadliest, merciless monster she had ever seen.

'Except not this!' yelled Antonio. 'Not this kind of unexpected, for God's sake!' He let out a bellow, throwing his hands up in the air as he stepped back. The glasses flew off the table and shattered on the floor. He screamed again. 'Noooo! Not tonight! Bloody hell!'

Sofia whimpered, crouching down as fast as she could and covering her head with her arms. Glasses had flown off the table with Terry too. Once he'd even smashed one into her chest. She'd told the doctor that she'd accidentally walked into a glass pane. What would happen next tonight? Trembling, she waited for the thump, the foot in her gut.

'Sofia?' gasped Antonio. 'Good God, what are you doing on the floor?'

She felt his hand on her arm, lifting her up. Was he making her stand only to kick her down again? That's what Terry used to do. If things didn't go his way, he'd take it out on her. How unlucky was she to have found another man just like her ex?

'Sofia, talk to me.' Antonio's fingers raised her chin. 'Look at me.'

She glanced at him for an instant before stepping away, her whole body shivering violently the way it used to when Terry threatened her. Or had hit her. It could take her hours to calm down after that, the contractions uncontrollable.

Antonio let out his breath. 'Just give me one second. I don't want to set the house on fire.' He rushed out of the room and a burnt smell filled the air. She heard a sizzling sound. Her mouth gaped. So that's why he'd screamed and gesticulated! He'd burnt the food.

When he returned to the dining room with rubber gloves, paper towel and a bag to clean up the broken glass, it was her cheeks that were on fire, not from embarrassment but from deep shame. He placed the paper towel and gloves on the table and came over to her. 'I'll clean up in a minute. Are you all right?'

She shrugged before quietly picking up her handbag, unable to look him in the eye.

'Sofia, what are you doing? You can't leave like this. I'm sorry I screamed and knocked the glasses off the table, waving my hands about like an idiot. You know what we're like in Italy, always talking with our hands. I've made a bloody mess of things. Look, I just so wanted to impress you tonight, and I forgot to turn off the osso buco. It had nothing to do with you. When I realised, I got mad and accidentally knocked the glasses off the table. You thought I was going to hit you, didn't you? I wasn't. Honestly.'

She rubbed her eyebrow. 'I ... I realise that now. I didn't understand at first.'

'I'd never hit you, Sofia. Never, ever, under any circumstances. You have to believe me.'

'I'm sorry, Antonio. I trust you as much as I can, as much as I'm capable of trust, but I just...' She was damaged goods. Terry had done this to her and she wasn't sure she'd ever manage to completely free herself from him, even now that he was no longer in her life.

'What happened to you, Sofia? Is this why you ended your marriage?'

She nodded slowly. 'I'm sorry I spoiled the evening.'

'It's OK. Tell me what happened with your ex. Tell me everything.'

Everything? How could she pronounce the words that she could barely whisper to herself? Conjure up images she wanted to forget? How did you justify staying two years with someone who made you feel like you were constantly walking on eggshells? Those who hadn't been through it themselves thought all you had to do was open the door and walk out. If only it were that simple. 'Maybe another time.' She turned to leave, her heart crushed.

'Please, Sofia, don't go. Stay with me. I'll make a salad or an omelette. We were having such a good time.'

They were, but the magic was broken now and it had become obvious to Sofia that she wasn't ready for this. She couldn't trust another man, certainly not yet. Perhaps she never would. 'It's better this way, Nino, believe me. I need to be alone. I can't be with you. I can't...' She couldn't do this to him. He deserved to be with someone who could trust him. 'I just can't do this. Please respect my decision.' The decision that broke her heart but was for the best. She had too little to give.

She dragged herself to the door, her limbs as heavy as blocks of concrete, and quietly closed it behind her as she slipped out into the night.

Chapter 11

Antonio stared at Sofia as they waited for the gastroenterologist to come to Nella's room and deliver his findings. Not once did she take her eyes off the floor, as if she couldn't stand to look at him since last night. Why had he gone and acted like an absolute idiot when he'd realised that he'd left the stove on and burned the osso buco? Damn it, he didn't sweat the small stuff—it wasn't his style—and he had to go and behave like that when he had Sofia over for dinner. He'd certainly never hurt her. He'd never laid a hand on a woman in his life and he wasn't about to start. He despised men who beat their partners.

That Sofia wouldn't meet his gaze now only made him want her more, *need* her more. Couldn't she see that it was too late, far too late for him to switch off and forget all about her? He hadn't forgotten her in all the years they'd been apart. What were the chances now? Nil. Less than that.

I love her more than anything.

He gasped at the realisation, the words resonating in his mind.

Nella pushed on her elbows, propping herself up in bed. 'Are you all right, Antonio? You look a little off.'

'*Si, si.* Just a little tired.' He'd had an early start, calling in at the butcher's, meeting the chief of staff and liaising with the team of field officers he'd been sent for the drop that was happening today, in just a few hours.

But that wasn't the reason. He'd only managed a couple of hours sleep as what had happened with Sofia that evening played over and over in his mind, and even then he'd woken in a cold sweat after dreaming that she'd fallen off a cliff before he could grab her hand and pull her to safety. Pull her to him, where she belonged.

And now his feelings towards her had taken him by surprise. He loved her. More than anything. Not as an excited starry-eyed teenager, but as the mature man that he was.

A balding fifty-something-year-old with a rounded belly entered. '*Buongiorno.* I'm Doctor Nobusso. I performed your sigmoidoscopy early this morning.'

'Yes, yes, I was in a daze but I remember you, doctor. *Buongiorno.*' Nella forced a smile, and Antonio wondered what was going through her mind. The awkwardness of knowing what the doctor had done? Worry about her condition? Whatever it was caused the tendons in her neck to tighten to the point of showing under her thinning skin. 'You can speak in front of my niece and our friend Antonio,' she said, clutching the sheet.

'Very well. It's all good news, as a matter of fact. As I suspected, it was a haemorrhoidal occurrence that appears to have mostly resolved itself. Other than that, there is nothing untoward in your bowel. This is about diet and hydration.' He handed her a leaflet. 'It's simple but important, especially in this heat. When your activity is limited you may not feel the need to drink, but you must.'

Sofia brought her hand to her forehead. 'Oh, my goodness. It's my fault. I should have been making you drink more.'

Nella shook her head. 'You're always offering me water, Sofia. I'm the one who leaves it on the table.' Antonio fought back the urge to place his hand on Sofia's back, to let her know he was there for her, that he wanted nothing more than to support her. But she'd been crystal clear the previous night. *I just can't do this. Please respect my decision.* The words that resonated in his mind twisted around his heart.

'So I don't need an operation for this, doctor?'

'It doesn't appear necessary at this stage and I'm hopeful that with good hydration and a high fibre diet it won't be needed later, either. There are always risks associated with an operation, especially later in life, so if it can be avoided, it's preferable. Any questions?'

A cheeky grin lit up Nella's face. 'When can I go home?'

'I'll organise your discharge late this afternoon. Just to make sure there are no complications following the mild anaesthetic you were given. They are very rare but in view of your age and medical condition, I don't want to take any chances.'

The specialist left and Nella raised her arms in the air. 'Thank you, God! It sounds like I'm going home tonight.'

'I can't wait!' Sofia patted her aunt's hand, grinning.

'I'm so pleased for you, Nella,' said Antonio coming close to the bed. He caught a whiff of Sofia's enticing scent as he stood behind her. He wanted to wallow in it, was dying to nuzzle against her neck. He moved to her side and sought her gaze. 'I'm pleased for you, too, Sofia. You must be so relieved. I know I am.'

She barely glanced at him. 'Yes, I am. Thank you, Antonio.'

He bit the inside of his cheek. This wasn't going to be easy. Perhaps it was just as well that he'd be out of her hair as he attended to the drop. He'd be gone for at least a few hours—and if things went awry, it could be days, maybe more if the mission turned into a catastrophe and he was injured again.

His stomach performed a somersault. Hell, being injured wasn't the worst that could happen. He knew that. He could be killed. Or worse, captured by the Mafia and tortured before being killed. But it was part of the deal, his job, his duty. He took a deep breath. 'I've a few things to do today,' he announced, watching Sofia from the corner of his eye. 'For work. There's no escaping it, I'm afraid.'

Sofia let out a long breath. Was she relieved that he'd be away? 'Sure. We understand. You mentioned it earlier.'

Nella shook her head. 'These jobs that won't leave you in peace during your holidays! It doesn't seem right, Antonio.'

He had said that it was a holiday 'of sorts'—he couldn't exactly tell them that he was more *in hiding, of sorts,* than on a true holiday. Anyway, the less they knew about it, the better. 'I'm hoping it will just be this afternoon, although it could go on for a while longer and I may be uncontactable. Please don't worry if that happens.'

'Uh-huh.' Sofia tilted her head. 'Like last time.' His shoulders tightened at the bitterness in her voice. Or was it simply calculated remoteness, now that she'd decided to keep her distance?

'Sofia!' Nella scolded her niece. 'You can't be annoyed because a man has a job to do.'

Sofia sighed. 'I'm sorry if I sounded annoyed. That wasn't my intention. I'm not at all annoyed because it's simply not my place to comment. It's not like Antonio is my boyfriend.'

The sadness in her eyes touched him. He smiled at her, his shoulders loosening. He was sorry to see her unhappiness and yet it was a relief to know that she felt *something* for him still. It meant she hadn't shut him out completely, didn't it? It meant that there was hope for him, hope for the two of them.

When he leaned closer to her, she finally looked into his eyes, and his stomach fell to his feet. Such beauty before him, such a sense of belonging with her, and he couldn't wrap his arms around her. 'It's fine, Sofia. You don't need to apologise. I completely understand.'

Her expression softened. Was that a touch of guilt on her face, even if she was doing her very best to seem uninterested and disengaged? Maybe ... He turned to the patient in her bed.

'So if I don't see you later today, enjoy being back in your own home, Nella.'

'That, I certainly will. Thank you for everything, Antonio. You've been an absolute angel for us, hasn't he, Sofia? A lifesaver.'

Sofia nodded shyly, wrapping her arms around her own waist. 'Thanks, Antonio,' she whispered.

'No trouble at all. It was my pleasure.' His absolute pleasure. In fact, he couldn't think of anyone he'd rather be with, even if he hated hospitals.

She gazed up at him with eyes full of emotion and if he'd been on his own with her, he might have reached out and pulled her to him. He might have pressed his lips to hers and sought her kiss one more time, burning inside from the desire that could so easily consume him if he gave in to it.

Except that he couldn't, not with Nella watching, and especially not when Sofia had told him that she needed to be alone and couldn't be with him. And he certainly couldn't now that he was about to drop off a heart and kidneys, that could so easily have been Nella's, to the Mafia. What if he didn't make it out alive?

That was a distinct possibility, so it was just as well that Sofia wouldn't be with him today, wouldn't kiss him today, wouldn't give her heart to him. He swallowed hard. Perhaps it was just as well that she didn't want to be with him at all. It was perfectly clear to him that she had suffered enough. The last thing she needed was to fall in love with someone whose life could be cut short at any moment by a bunch of gangsters and Antonio's life certainly could. It was a sobering thought.

He wanted nothing more than Sofia, he still hoped that she would find her way into the warmth of his arms, but maybe the right thing to do, after all, at the very least until he had closed the organ smuggling case, was to leave her in peace and respect her need to be alone.

Shame every fibre of his being rebelled against the idea.

***

Sofia watched Nella as her chest rose and dropped with each deep breath. Her aunt was certainly catching up on sleep now, finally able to relax after this morning's good news. Haemorrhoids! Sofia smiled. Such an easy fix. If only everything was so simple.

Her gaze fell on the chair that Antonio had appropriated earlier and her heart sank. She wished he were still there, on it, so that she could feel his eyes on her again and the way they burned right through to her heart.

But she still had trust issues and at his house when Antonio had thrown his hands in the air and screamed at the burnt dinner, she'd followed her gut. It had been an uncontrollable reaction, like that of a soldier who'd heard a bang after coming back from a war-torn country. There was no doubt she'd been scared, but was she really so damaged that she couldn't try again with any man? Had she overreacted? Could she find a way to control those impulses? If she got help, would it work?

She wasn't sure, but she wouldn't find out by pushing Antonio away too soon.

She stood and gazed through the hospital window at the tree-lined carpark, and further down the street to the small park between two apartment blocks. There were people there, walking side-by-side beneath the umbrella pines, and yet the world seemed empty, as empty as Sofia's heart. A beautiful plant had been putting down root in the garden of her life and as it was about to bloom it had been abruptly pulled out by an unscrupulous gardener.

She sat back down with a sigh. *She* was the unscrupulous gardener. She listened to her aunt's regular breaths, the only sound in the silent room. No deep, chocolate voice to send shivers from her head down to her toes. No warm laughter to brighten her mood, no fleeting touch of the most protective hand she'd ever felt. Antonio was gone—she'd talked herself into believing it was better if he left her alone—and now she ached for him.

She closed her eyes and it was almost as if she could smell his scent, feel the heat of his body behind her. Almost as if all she had to do was turn around, offer him her lips and give this man, and herself, another chance.

The urge to hear his voice was greater than any she'd known. She rummaged through her handbag for her phone and dialled his number. It went directly to voicemail. 'Hello, Antonio. It's Sofia. I, hmm ... I just wanted to...' She sighed. 'All is well. No need to worry. I'll try you again later.' She hung up.

What was he doing? Sitting at a desk discussing issues on a conference call, unable to answer? In the middle of taking notes as he listened? Or was work just an excuse and he was out enjoying himself because he'd had enough of the hospital and in any case Sofia had made it clear to him that she didn't want to be with him, or with any man for that matter? Could he be out seducing someone else?

She rubbed her forehead, pushing away the thought. Her stupid lack of trust was making her think that way, the things that her ex had done had conditioned her. But she could beat those, she could beat Terry and the world of fear, pain and submission he'd inflicted on her. That was all in the past and Antonio was different.

Yes, she'd made a mistake last night. She'd been wrong to push Antonio away. If she talked to him now, if she explained her fears, her past, that she needed to take things slowly—and that certain triggers like raising your hands and screaming were best avoided—he'd understand, wouldn't he? He'd give her another shot, right? She hoped so with all her heart.

She picked up her phone and called him again. It rang and rang, before finally going to voicemail once more. This time, she didn't know what to say. 'Me again. Sorry to bother you. Maybe it's better if you call me when you can.' She hung up, her heart heavy. Five minutes on the phone with him was all she wanted, but he was busy.

Not being able to reach him now was getting to her, even if it shouldn't. She was impatient to hear his voice, impatient to try and fix the mess she'd made and remove the noose that hung around her neck. The grey hospital walls, plastic visitor chairs and neon lighting suddenly oppressed her. How long had she been here, in this drab room? She had to get out, had to get away for a while.

She found a piece of paper in her handbag and scribbled a note to Nella. *Gone for a drive. Will be back later in the afternoon. Love you. xxx*

Where would Antonio be working? From a nearby café? His work could be sensitive. More likely from home. Yes, he'd have gone back to Sant'Agosto for sure. Perhaps he'd switched his phone off so as not to be interrupted. Perhaps he'd left it in another room. The best way to find out was to call in at his place. Not for long, just a few minutes, as she knew he was busy. But a few minutes would make all the difference to her. Perhaps to him, too, if he felt as devastated as she did about what had happened last night between them.

She hurried out of Nella's room, down the corridor and to the lifts. As the bell sounded and she stepped in, she remembered how Antonio's scent had filled her lungs the first time they'd found themselves in this very lift together. And how her heart had pounded in her chest. She hadn't been able to send him away then, hadn't been able to refuse his invitation to share a meal. The attraction between them was so powerful. It always had been, even if things had gone wrong. She hurried through the ground floor and out into the heat of the day, climbing into her aunt Nella's red-hot car, wishing it had air-conditioning. She opened both front windows and drove off, happy to see the ochre-coloured buildings, their green shutters and the brilliant blue sky.

Thankfully the drive to the hospital was straightforward, and she could find her way back to Sant'Agosto without a GPS, which she didn't have the luxury of in Nella's old bomb. All Sofia had to do was turn left at the T-junction onto the main road, follow it to via Falcone, the street with the big concrete crucifix on the corner, turn right there, and then at the next junction Sant'Agosto was clearly indicated.

As she came to via Falcone she slowed to turn, and then hit the brakes when she saw the narrow, rather upmarket street, lined with perfectly maintained elaborate facades of a number of small buildings that were no doubt home to the wealthiest in Cassone, had been cordoned off for roadworks. 'Bummer! Now what?' She only knew one way home. She pulled over onto the side of the road. She'd rummage around the glove box in the hope of finding a map, and if she didn't, she'd have to ask someone for directions. There was nothing of use to her in the glove box, so she climbed out of the car to seek help.

As she glanced down the street she noticed someone towards the other end of via Falcone, no doubt a resident as no cars were allowed to pass through there today. And then a tall, strong silhouette caught her eye as it stepped out of one of the properties, through a heavy wooden door that seemed fit for a castle. It was a silhouette she knew well, and her heart skipped a beat. Antonio? Was it him? She squinted and looked again. Yes, there was no doubt about it. What was he doing there?

A woman appeared behind him, hurried to his side and playfully pulled him to her. Antonio let her, there in the street in broad daylight, in front of the three men who were digging, fixing something in the pavement, and the other man standing further ahead with a box in hand. Pain shot through Sofia's stomach, robbing her of her breath. How could Antonio do this, not even twenty-four hours after he'd invited Sofia over for a romantic dinner? After the intensity between them, the way they were drawn to each other?

Rage bubbled in her veins and concentrated in her chest. If he thought he was going to get away with it, he had another thing coming. She wasn't about to call out to him, wasn't going to yell in his direction. She wanted to get closer, up close and personal in fact, to see the look in his eyes when he suddenly realised that she was watching. Was this the kind of *work* he'd been doing when Sofia had hurt her ankle and he'd disappeared for days without a word, although he'd promised to come and help Nella? It must have been.

Sofia marched up the street in his direction. She wasn't sorry she was here. She wasn't sorry she'd spotted him.

Her only regret was that she'd been about to trust him with her heart.

Chapter 12

Everything was in place. The workers digging up the street, who were none other than three of the best officers on Antonio's team, had guns hidden under a fine layer of dirt. Officer Luca Tizzo, who, because of his similar looks, was impersonating Chief of Staff Rinotto with a box in hand that contained the heart and kidneys of a pig, stood towards the end of the street waiting for the fake ambulance that had been spotted by other plain-clothed carabinieri posted for surveillance half a kilometre away. Antonio had been informed that it was about to arrive within two to three minutes. And Marta Caccia, the woman hanging happily off his arm, was the best elite shooter in Italy. If anything went wrong, she had orders to kill if necessary, orders from Commander Carone himself.

Antonio steeled himself. Nothing would go wrong. None of his men would die. For a split second an image of Sofia breaking down when an officer announced Antonio's death to her, flashed through his mind. He sighed as he and Marta stepped out of the house that had been requisitioned and in which they'd been hiding, waiting for exactly the right moment to make their appearance.

'What?' Marta snapped in her usual harsh manner, before smiling and leaning her head against his shoulder.

'Nothing.' He smiled back. 'The truth is, I hope no civilians turn up. Doing the drop here instead of somewhere more remote is making me nervous. They must be trying to get the organs somewhere nearby really fast.'

'Nevertheless you need to relax and come closer. You'll get us both killed if you keep acting nervous and they recognise you.' She snuggled up to him, her hair half covering Antonio's face.

An ambulance pulled into the street from the opposite end and two men climbed out, heading straight to Luca.

'We won't get killed. You're here to save the day, aren't you, sweet Marta?' Antonio chuckled, knowing full well that Marta couldn't always perform miracles even if she never missed her target. And she certainly wasn't sweet.

She laughed, loud and clear, as if Antonio had been whispering cheeky promises into her ear. She wasn't just a good shot, she was a good actress, pretending very convincingly to be in love with him.

The ambulance men glanced their way, but dismissed their presence, nodding to Luca and gesturing to the box he held.

'Get them to talk,' whispered Antonio into the tiny microphone on the pen in his shirt pocket.

'How do I know who you are?' Luca asked, his words transmitted back to Antonio through the wire he was wearing.

'You know exactly who we are. We had an appointment, remember? For that box. Now hand it over.'

'The box with two hearts and a kidney?'

'Are you fucking with us?'

'Oh, I'm sorry, two kidneys and a heart. I'm nervous. You can't blame me for that. I'm chief of staff at the local hospital. I'm not used to giving away organs to the Mafia. That's what this is, isn't it? I like to know who I'm dealing with.'

One of the men pointed a gun at Luca from under his jacket, glancing quickly once again towards Antonio and Marta. 'Shut the fuck up and gimme that, unless you want to be chopped into pieces and shoved in that box too.'

'Do as he says, Luca,' blurted Antonio into his pen, still walking in Luca's direction. 'Stay calm. Now give them the box before they get too worked up.'

'Yeah, or he'll get his brains blown next,' mumbled Marta.

Luca put the box on the ground and slid it over their way.

Suddenly, a hand tugged at Antonio's shoulder and spun him around. His mouth fell open when he saw Sofia standing there, rage in her eyes.

'Sofia, my God!' His only thought was what would happen if she were somehow caught in this mission, hurt, or worse. 'It's not what you think.'

'Oh, yeah?' Her cheeks were as red as the cross on the box that the Mafia was picking up. Her arm pulled back, gathering strength, and her hand came so close to his cheek that he could feel the heat from it. She took it away without slapping him, forming a fist instead.

'I'll neutralise her,' hissed Marta, raising a fist ready to knock the wind out of Sofia.

'Marta, no! It's an order.' Antonio latched onto Marta's arm, holding it back. The last thing he needed was to draw attention to the two women while Luca was dealing with the Mafiosi.

'That's right, Mr Big Shot. Tell all your chicks what to do.' Sofia was yelling now, trembling like a leaf ready to fall off a tree. 'Last night, if you hadn't burned the food, we would have been in bed. And today you say you have to go to work when you're parading around with some woman. You heard me, lady, he would have cheated on you, too, last night, if I'd let him. Antonio De

Santis, you are a disgusting, filthy pig. What am I saying? Compared to you, pigs are adorable.'

Antonio turned to check on the ambulance men, at the same time as they stared at him. 'Fuck! It's a set-up!' yelled one of them, probably recognising Antonio, and the Mafiosi both pulled out their guns while running back to the ambulance, the box in hand.

Luca fumbled for his gun, half crouching down, while Marta aimed calmly at the first man and took the shot.

Meanwhile, one of the Mafiosi aimed at Sofia. 'Hey, De Santis, this is for your bitch and you!'

'No!' screamed Antonio, throwing himself in front of her and pushing her out of the way so hard that she seemed to fly through the air.

In that instant, pain rushed through his body and he had no idea where it originated. He was all pain, nothing but pain, every single one of his nerve endings on high alert, the agony robbing him of his breath.

He fell to his knees, aware only of how cold he suddenly became, and he wanted to scream, he wanted to cry, but even tears seemed to require more energy than was left in him.

And then Antonio's world turned black.

Pitch black, as if someone had switched him off.

His last thought was that Sofia had to make it out alive.

***

Sofia had never seen that much blood in her life. It formed a pool around the two men who had shot in her direction, presumably criminals. And Antonio's shirt was soaked with his own precious blood, thick and red.

She'd never seen a person die before, and the last thing she wanted was to watch Antonio take his last breath. She'd rather have taken the bullet herself than see that happen. What had she done? Antonio had thrown himself in front of her to protect her, when she was the one who'd messed up their mission and now he was bleeding from the chest. She'd doubted him so many times and everything had been true. *Oh, God*, what had she done?

The tall woman Antonio had called Marta had dealt with the bad guys. At some stage, the three road workers who'd been digging holes in the asphalt had come running down the street and joined in. Sofia couldn't quite get her head around how they'd also come rushing up with guns in their hands, unless ... Of course, they too must have been working with Antonio. The cordoned off street had been part of the set-up as well.

She'd mistaken an undercover operation for a normal, daily scene, one in which she'd jumped to the conclusion that Antonio was in a relationship with Marta. She hadn't once stopped to think that he might have been working, that this might have been field work that he couldn't mention to her. Her feelings of betrayal and jealousy had prevailed over reason and now she'd give anything to take back her actions.

What she wanted most of all was to save the man whose life she'd put at risk, the man she sat slumped next to on the road. The most precious man in the world. She hadn't yet told him that he mattered to her more than any man ever had.

He was still alive, wasn't he?

Please, dear God, let him be alive. I'm sorry. I'm so sorry. Take what you want from me. Take anything, as long as he lives.

His eyes were shut tight and his skin had turned a pasty white. Was he still breathing? She couldn't even tell through her tears. Suddenly his eyelids flickered, and then he gazed at her for a split second. 'Sofia ... Are you hit?'

Before she could answer, his eyes rolled back, he let out a low rumble and then ... nothing.

'Antonio. Antonio!'

She tilted his head back to make sure his airways were clear, and when his mouth opened she lifted his chin. She folded his arm and leg, putting him into the recovery position. It was what she remembered from the last time she'd done first aid training.

Marta came over and kneeled beside Antonio, shooting Sofia a frosty glance.

'I can't feel his pulse anymore,' blurted Sofia, not bothering to wipe the tears rolling down her cheeks.

Antonio's icy colleague placed her fingers against his neck.

'Is he going to be OK?' asked Sofia. 'Please tell me he's going to be OK.'

'I can't say.' Marta stood, towering above Sofia. 'I think he's been shot in the lung.'

'We need an ambulance,' mumbled Sofia. 'Can't we take that one?'

'The fake one with no equipment and no staff? Smart move.'

Sofia trembled from head to toe. 'We have to save him.'

'Put your hands on the wound and press. It will slow the blood loss.'

Sofia obeyed, holding both hands on the bullet entry point on Antonio's chest, and watched her fingers become red with Antonio's blood. Her head spun and her stomach heaved, but she wasn't about to let either of those things stop her from helping this brave, caring, heavenly man. The man who meant more to her than any other could, ever since she was barely out of childhood.

Marta took out her phone and dialled. 'Officer down. We urgently need an ambulance corner of via Falcone and via Centrale. You'll see an ambulance when you get here. Ignore it, it's a fake one. We also have two...' Her voice faded as she walked away, turning her back to Sofia in what seemed to be cold anger. Or was the woman simply devoid of all feelings? Sofia wasn't sure, and it didn't matter. The only thing that mattered was saving Antonio. Nino. Her Nino.

Her tears fell onto his pale face. 'I'm so sorry, Antonio. This is all my fault. How could I be so stupid? Please don't die. Please, please don't leave me. I don't think I could live without you.'

At that moment, his hand moved a little. She looked down at it, wondering if she'd imagined it, but he did it again. His little finger wriggled.

Sofia laughed through her tears. 'Thank you, God, he's still alive. Thank you, Antonio, for letting me know. You're going to make it.' And if life gave her a second chance, and Antonio did too, she, too, would make it out of the darkness Terry had got her used to, and into the light that shone wherever Antonio went.

A siren sounded in the distance. 'The ambulance is coming, it'll be here soon. Hold on, sweetheart.' *Sweetheart.* That, he was for sure. His heart was sweet and courageous and unshakeable. He was kind and smart and amazing. He'd taken the bullet that was meant for her. What more could she want? What more could she need?

Forgiveness. She needed him to be forgiving, to forgive *her*, to live through this and give her another chance. Was it too much to ask? It was an awful lot to ask, she knew that much, yet she was asking anyway, praying anyway. She'd have sold her soul for it.

An ambulance—a real one this time—pulled up at the end of the street. 'Hang on, honey, help is here.'

Two paramedics came running towards Antonio with a stretcher, and lifted him onto it. They hurried him back to the vehicle, pulled in one of the Mafiosi, and then another ambulance arrived and parked near the remaining criminal who lay in a pool of blood.

Sofia tried to climb into the ambulance with Antonio, but the paramedic who was now placing an oxygen mask on him stopped her. 'Sorry, we're full house here. You're going to have to find another ride to the hospital.'

She nodded, resting her hand on Antonio's foot for an instant. 'You'll be all right, darling. You're going to make it. *We're* going to make it, if it's the last thing I do. I'll see you at the hospital.'

As the doors of the ambulance closed shut with a bang, she hoped that he had heard her. And that she was right about them surviving this together.

Because she simply couldn't bear the thought of being wrong about it and losing the most wonderful man in the world.

***

Sofia walked the full length of the waiting room and back, before starting again. How many times had she paced up and down in the hope of seeing a doctor emerge and bring her news of Antonio? She'd lost count.

Marta had stayed for a while but then she'd received a phone call and had to disappear. Sofia hadn't asked why—she knew better than to stick her nose where it didn't belong now, after having messed up the *carabinieri's* sting. But she'd promised to send Antonio's colleague an SMS as soon as there was news about his condition, and

Marta had assured her that she would pass the information onto all those concerned.

Finally, a doctor appeared, the dark circles under his eyes no doubt a sign of his exhaustion and the excessive demands of his job. Lives depended on him. That couldn't be easy. 'Signorina Conti?'

'Yes, doctor.' Her words came out like a husky whisper, as if the huge lump in her throat had squeezed them dry as they passed by it.

'The *carabinieri* have asked me to inform you of progress with respect to *il signore* De Santis.'

As the doctor paused, so did Sofia's heart. She took a deep breath, and the doctor, who must have noticed, quickly continued. 'The bullet has perforated his lung. We are lucky that it happened so close to the hospital, that he was brought in so quickly and that the paramedics performed a needle decompression on the way. We've removed the bullet, were able to stop the bleeding and he is now stable.'

Joy filled Sofia's heart and she let out a cry of relief. 'Thank you, doctor. Thank you so much.' She placed her hand in front of her mouth, barely able to believe the words the man in the white coat had uttered.

'He's out of the woods, Ms Conti, but I have to warn you that it will be a long road to total recovery, usually between one and three months, if not more. Still, he's in excellent physical condition and I am hopeful that he will reach that point, and sooner rather than later.'

'And if not?'

'There can be complications. But let's cross that bridge if and when we get to it.'

Sofia nodded. It was a sobering thought that it could take so long, and even more so that there could be difficulties along the way, but still, to know that he was generally speaking out of the woods was a gift that lightened her shoulders, her mood, her heart. 'I'll do whatever it takes for him to get better.'

'You should start by making sure he has a lot of rest.'

'No problem.' Was it really no problem with someone like Antonio? A man of action, responsibility, a man who risked his life for the community. It was probably going to be a hell of a lot trickier than just telling him to take it easy.

'You will have to convince him to stay out of trouble for quite a while. Work is off the cards, especially in his line of duty. He can't make it a habit of taking bullets like this.'

'Sorry? A habit?' How many bullets had he taken in the past? Did the doctor know something Sofia didn't?

He looked away. 'Hmm, we wouldn't want this to happen again.'

'I'll do my very best to keep him safe, doctor.' She meant it. She owed Nino big time, but more than that, she wanted nothing more in the world than for him to be happy and healthy again. To be happy and healthy *with her*. 'When can I see him?'

'He's sleeping now. It will be quite a few more hours before the effects of the anaesthetic start to wear off. You ought to go home and perhaps come back in the morning. There's nothing more we can do for him at this time, and he's in good hands. We are monitoring him carefully. If there's any change in his condition we have your number. And the men that were sent in are diligently guarding his door.'

Sofia took a deep breath at the reminder that Antonio had security in front of his room. Security that meant he was still in danger. 'I can't go home just yet as my aunt is in the hospital too. Hopefully, she's being discharged today, though, and then we'll head back.'

'Sounds like you've been having a bad run. Well, I hope all goes well with your aunt too.'

As he was about to turn away, she stopped him. 'Excuse me, doctor, the other two men that came in at the same time?' Had the men that Marta shot survived? Would they be paying for their crimes in jail? Or helping the police in their inquiries? Or were they completely out of the picture and facing Judgement Day in another world?

'I'm afraid I'm not at liberty to say, but put it this way, they're not getting off that easily. And they're not a threat to Mr De Santis at this time.'

She nodded her thanks and as soon as the doctor took his leave, she whipped out her phone and wrote to Marta.

He's stable, out of the woods, thank heavens. I'm so relieved, and so sorry about my behaviour, the misunderstanding. I've been such a fool. Thanks for everything, Marta. I owe you. Without Antonio's frosty colleague who'd shot the bad guys, Antonio might not be here at all and others might have died too.

The response came almost instantly and wasn't nearly as cold as Sofia had expected. *Apology accepted. Just doing my job. Glad to hear about De Santis. Thanks for the update. I'll pass it onto Commander Carone.*

Sofia shot off another text. *Sounds like the other two men have pulled through, although the doctor isn't allowed to say too much.*

Scum. But I didn't aim to kill, only to put them out of action—and make them suffer. Again, just doing my job.

Sofia raised her eyebrows. Marta wanted the men to live? *You didn't want to kill them?*

Dead scum don't talk ☺ *Ciao, Sofia. Stay out of trouble.*

Sofia smiled. She had no doubt Marta would be successful at making any scum talk, as long as there was the tiniest bit of life left in them.

As she headed down the corridor to the lift that she would take up to Nella's floor she rubbed her forehead. How was she going to tell Nella about Antonio? It would certainly put a dampener on her lovely aunt's discharge. Perhaps she ought to spare the old woman who'd had enough to cope with lately, and withhold the news until he was conscious.

After all, there wasn't anything Nella could do to help Antonio.

All any of them could do right now was wait and hope for the best.

Chapter 13

Antonio struggled to open his eyes. When he finally managed to glance at his surroundings he seemed to recognise Nella's hospital room.

What the hell am I doing here? Did I doze off?

He tried to move but pain nailed him to the bed. Memories of the drop, Marta nuzzled against his neck, came flooding back.

Shot. I think I was shot.

That's right. It suddenly made sense. He was the patient now, not Nella. He groaned as he wondered what his injuries might be. It was worse than last time, when the bullet had just grazed him. It hurt a lot more. At least he was still alive. Panic spread through his body, clawing its way up his chest to his throat as his mind became clearer. Sofia had come to via Falcone as the fake ambulance had arrived to pick up the heart and kidneys that Luca carried in a box. Antonio had survived the shootings, but what about Sofia? Although he thought he'd heard her talking to him when he'd blacked out, he might have been dreaming.

'Sofia...' he murmured through parched lips.

'I'm right here, Antonio.' The hand that pressed his softly put an end to his worst fear.

'You're OK?' With effort, he turned his head and saw that she wasn't in a bed. He managed to discern her beautiful features, too, although his vision was somewhat blurred. 'You made it. Good. You're stronger than me.'

She laughed in response to his comment, but it wasn't the joyful, bubbly laughter that usually warmed his heart so much. It was the kind of chuckle that people hide behind, the nervous giggle they pull over worry, embarrassment and raw wounds like a blanket. 'Stronger than you?' she asked. 'I don't think so. You saved me and now I'm the first thing you worry about instead of wondering what's wrong with you. You're amazing, you know that? Yes, I'm fine, but the important thing is that you made it too, Antonio.'

He blinked her into focus and stared at her gorgeous face, those red lips he wanted to kiss even from his hospital bed, those kind eyes brimming with tears he wanted to wipe away. 'So what is wrong with me, now that you mention it?' He steeled himself. What if she told him that he wasn't ever going to be the man he once was? What if he was doomed to hospital care, machines, completely incapacitated? A chill spread through him.

'You were shot in the lung. But you're going to be all right. You can make a full recovery, the doctor's assured me, as long as you rest.

They'll come and give you all the details, I'm sure. Do you want me to go and see if I can get someone now to explain it all?'

He shook his head, while a smile crept onto his lips. A full recovery was possible. That's all he needed to know. If it was possible, he'd make it happen. 'The debrief can wait. I'd rather spend time with you than some nerdy surgeon. How long have I been here?'

'Nearly twenty-four hours.'

A whole day and he had no idea. 'I've lost a day of my life? Crap.'

Sofia leaned over the bed and brushed the hair off his forehead. 'You haven't lost anything. Your body has been busy recovering, rebuilding. That's time well spent if you ask me.'

He made a sound of reluctant acquiescence. 'I suppose so. My boss? Commander Carone?'

'Marta's been liaising with him.'

The always efficient Marta. He thanked his lucky stars for her. 'I'm really thirsty.'

Sofia filled a glass with water and brought it to his lips, cupping his head in her free hand. He sipped carefully, the cool liquid trickling down to his stomach.

'Were you injured?' he asked once he'd had enough to drink. 'I had to shove you out of the way. The last thing I saw was you flying towards the pavement.'

'No, just a couple of bruises. I'm absolutely fine, and it's all because of you. You saved my life, Antonio. You took a bullet for me. Thank you so much.' She let out a pained sigh. 'Saying thank you seems so little in exchange for what you did.'

He winced as he shrugged, the slightest movement hurting his chest. 'I couldn't have lived with the idea that you'd been killed because of me, Sofia.' He knew it in his soul. If she'd been caught in the crossfire, or shot dead by one of the Mafiosi, he never would have forgiven himself, never would have found joy in life again.

She rubbed her forehead before speaking. 'The thing is, Antonio, if I'd died it wouldn't have been because of you, whereas the opposite is true. What happened was all my fault. I never should have come after you. I never should have interfered. And I never should have doubted anything you said to me.'

He smiled and held out his hand. She pulled her chair closer and slipped her fingers around his before continuing to speak. 'I was actually driving to your house because I thought that's where you'd be working. And then I saw you there in the street, coming out of a private building with another woman on your arm and I don't know what happened to me. I snapped. That's it. I just went crazy. I couldn't stand the idea of you being with her when the night before, you'd invited me over for a romantic dinner. I couldn't stand the thought of you being a liar like that. Not that you owe me anything. We aren't together. It's stupid ... *I'm* stupid.'

Her cheeks reddened and she covered her face with her hands. 'And I nearly slapped you. God, I never expected to try to slap anyone in my life. I never have before.'

'Sofia, let it go.' He hated seeing the guilt in her eyes. 'You didn't know what was going on. It's just unfortunate that you drove by at the time we were doing the drop. I did tell you I was working.'

She wrung her hands. 'I know you did. And I know I'm in the wrong. I just thought you meant working on a document at home, so when I saw you with your colleague in plain clothes it didn't click.' She stood, walking around the room like a caged animal. 'I hate that I jumped to conclusions like that. I hate that I've become like that. I need to tell you about Terry, my ex-husband. I should have the other night, but I just couldn't. I'll tell you everything when you're feeling better.'

'Tell me now. I want to know.' He nodded to encourage her. If he'd been able to stand close to her and draw her to him, to hold her against his body and rub her back to soothe her, he would have.

'OK. When I thought I wouldn't ever find anyone to settle down with, Terry came along. He was charming and very attentive. In fact, his whole world seemed to revolve around me. He wrote me love letters and always wanted to know what I was thinking. It was too much, but I didn't notice that at first. I was too happy to have finally found someone who seemed so taken by me that he knew straight away that he wanted to spend his life with me.'

Antonio's jaw tightened. Terry wasn't the first to feel that way about Sofia. Antonio was. He'd always known that she was the one. Why hadn't she given him a chance when they were young?

For that very reason. You were young and so was she. Too young.

'He asked me to marry him, didn't want us to move in together without doing things properly, he said. It was a whirlwind romance, one that was too good to be true, with roses and candlelit dinners and special boxed gifts. He made me feel like a princess, and I accepted his proposal. But soon after we were married, Terry started bossing me around. He had a gun that he played with at times, especially if I seemed reluctant to do something he wanted me to.

There was this underlying threat, this hidden fear and I was walking on eggshells day and night. He told me what to do, when to do it and how he wanted it done. He even had me fold the towels a certain way. And if I didn't comply, he'd turn into a screaming madman.'

Antonio's heart ached. To hear those things, to see the agony on her face as she relived the moments and her eyes brimming with tears, was breaking him. He patted the bed. 'Sofia, come sit next to me.' She hesitated. *'Please.'*

Her head down, she slowly perched on the bed next to him. He held out his hand again and she squeezed it briefly. But she quickly let go, crossing her arms before continuing her story. 'Terry soon turned to throwing things when he wasn't happy. Vases, glasses.'

Like the ones Antonio had knocked off the dinner table, albeit unintentionally. He moaned.

'Are you all right?'

'Yes. It's not pain. I'm just mortified I smashed those glasses and scared you when you came over. Please, go on.'

'One night, when dinner was ten minutes late, he saw that a package had been delivered to the house, a cardigan I'd ordered online. He said he'd noticed the postman was a young, handsome guy, and he accused me of having spent the afternoon with him. I'd never even said hello to the postie, never even looked at the man.

'That night, Terry stood in front of the mirror in the hallway, talking to himself under his breath. I asked him what was wrong and he said I should know, that I'd been sleeping with the postman. When I said he was imagining things, that he was going crazy, he grabbed me by the hair and flung me into the wall.'

'I'm so sorry, Sofia.' He couldn't begin to imagine how betrayed she must have felt on top of the physical trauma.

'The next day my husband came home with a huge bunch of flowers and asked me for forgiveness. He said he got carried away, that it wouldn't happen again, that he loved me more than anything in the world. After that, I saw Terry talking to himself in front of the mirror like a madman on more than one occasion. I tried to leave, but he threatened to kill me and everyone I'd ever cared about. It took me two years to free myself of him. You probably think I'm weak.'

'Not at all. I think you're very brave for having stood up to him.'

She wiped a tear with the back of her hand. 'Apparently, I'm one of the lucky ones. It takes many women decades to get away, and then there are all those who never make it out alive.'

'I get it. You don't have to worry about me judging you, Sofia. I've seen violence. I know how it takes its prisoners.' That was one of the main reasons Mafia spouses stayed, one of the reasons no one ever talked or walked. 'I so wish I could hold you right now. Thank you for explaining all this. I understand completely why you reacted the way you did when I yelled about the dinner I'd burned and smashed the glasses. I want you to know that I'd never, ever hurt you. I'd never even threaten you. You know that, right?'

She nodded timidly. 'I do. You saved my life, Antonio. If I can't trust you, then I can't trust anyone.'

He smiled when he wanted nothing more than to pick her up, spin her around in his arms and scream to the world that he loved her. He loved her more than life itself. Why else would he throw himself in front of her when a bullet was flying her way? It wasn't just because it was his duty to do so.

It was because he needed her more than oxygen.

Was it more oxygen that he needed, too, to stop the sudden urge he had to close his eyes and drift off to sleep again? He didn't know. All he knew was that he couldn't resist, couldn't fight his body. 'I'm so tired,' he whispered.

'It's fine, you go back to sleep. You need all the rest you can get.'

'Nella?' he asked, remembering that twenty-four hours had gone by since he'd had any news of her and that she was meant to be discharged from hospital.

'She's home and loving it. In fact, she's quite lively. I've been back briefly a couple of times today and Marisa, the local general practitioner's daughter, is there to help out. You remember Marisa?'

'Hmm. I do. One more thing.' He fought hard to keep his eyes open.

'Yes?'

'Why were you coming to my house?'

She drew a sharp breath. 'Because I realised I'd made a mistake by pushing you away. I shouldn't have just left when you got upset about burning the food. I should have tried harder to explain about Terry. I shouldn't have given up that easily. And now I know I should have trusted you a whole lot more.' Sofia's fingers landed on his forehead and gently swept the hair off his face. 'I should have trusted you completely.'

His heart nearly burst with pleasure at her confession. 'You have no idea how happy it makes me to hear that, Sofia. If I wasn't stuck in a hospital bed...' He would have whispered words of desire to her, kissed her from head to toe, and made sweet love to her for hours if she'd let him. And by the sound of things, one of these days she might just do that. But he was in no condition to even think about those magic moments and he was struggling more than ever to stay awake. 'I'm really sorry, I'm falling asleep.'

'Don't be sorry. After everything you've been through, and all the stuff they're pumping into your body, I'm surprised you've managed to talk this long. Thrilled about it too.'

'Not as thrilled as me.' To know that she had survived, that he had too, and that life could be good again, together with Sofia, made him the happiest man on earth. His eyes closed once more and his head rolled heavily to the side. 'I'm not going to be good company for much longer. Why don't you go home, Sofia? Give Nella a hug from me?'

'All right, I might do that. You have men in front of your door to keep you safe. They were sent by your unit.'

Men in front of his hospital room ... Of course, he was still in danger. 'The two men from the ambulance who were shooting? Are they dead?'

'Apparently not. That's good, right? You'll be able to get information out of them.'

His head hurt, his chest hurt, and sleep was dragging him into the world of dreams. Still, he managed a nod. 'Be careful, Sofia,' he mumbled, pushing through the pain and the exhaustion. 'If you see anything unusual, stay away. Don't talk to strangers. Just go straight home, don't stop on the way. I need to ask for men to protect your home too. I couldn't bear to lose you. I need you, Sofia.'

She smiled at him, her eyes twinkling. 'I need you too.'

He fumbled about helplessly.

'What are you doing, Antonio? What do you want?'

'Phone. I have to get you some protection.'

'It's OK. I'll sort it out. I have Marta's number. I'll contact her. Leave it with me.'

His eyelids were as heavy as lead. It must have been the drugs he'd been given. All he could do was grunt in response and take one last look at Sofia's beautiful face.

'Don't worry. You don't need to worry about anything except getting better.'

But his last thought before darkness fell upon him once more was that he did have to worry. In fact, if Sofia was with him, if they became a couple like he so desired and she now seemed to want as much as he did, he would have an awful lot to worry about, all the time.

Because he'd be putting Sofia in danger, in serious, constant danger, the kind that gave you nightmares. The kind that made you incapable of ensuring the safety of those you loved, and made waking up in a cold sweat part of your ordinary existence.

Sofia didn't need to live in fear.

She'd had enough of that already to last a lifetime with that bastard she'd married before.

Antonio certainly wouldn't be the one to inflict that kind of suffering upon her again because he loved her and he simply couldn't do that to her. As much as he wanted her, he couldn't bring her into this life run by the Mafia.

Chapter 14

Sofia couldn't remember the last time she'd felt so light, as if every problem in the world had vanished. It wasn't the case, of course. Troubles lay ahead for her as for every living being, as sure as the air she breathed. Life was never simple for very long, and Antonio had a long recovery ahead of him, as well as a dangerous job. And then there was poor Nella, who was home and feeling better, but she wasn't cured.

Yet Sofia couldn't stop smiling, all the while humming a happy tune, and it had nothing to do with the good night's sleep she'd had.

'You're very chirpy,' said Nella from the couch where she'd been sipping apple juice—sitting up, instead of lying down as usual.

'Well, it's lovely to have you back home and you seem better than you've been in a long time. I mean, look at you, *zia* Nella, sitting up to drink without any help whatsoever.' It was true, and Sofia was sincerely thrilled by Nella's improvement, although it wasn't the only reason she couldn't wipe the grin off her face.

The other reason was that Antonio was alive. He'd pull through this, she was sure. The doctors were as confident as the medical profession could ever be that he would make a full recovery. And she'd talked to him and told him everything, about Terry, about her fears, about her feelings. Progress had been made. Real, solid progress.

Nella put down her glass of juice. 'It's lovely to be home and I'm touched that you're pleased to have me back. Your eyes are sparkling with so much happiness, you look like you might have won the lottery. Are you sure there isn't anything else you want to tell me?'

Sofia took a deep breath as she pulled up a chair by her aunt. She still had the awful task of telling her aunt about Antonio's injury and that she was responsible for it. 'There is, actually, but before the good news, I probably should give you the bad.'

Nella sat forward, determination in her eyes. 'Whatever it is, just say it, Sofia. I'll be all right. They've given you sobering news about me?'

Sofia held up her hand to signal that Nella needn't worry about that. 'No, nothing like that. It's about Antonio.'

'Antonio? You've argued?'

'No, *zia*. In fact, it's quite the opposite. We seem to be getting along better than ever. Actually, I'm positive about that.'

Nella threw her hands in the air with a chuckle. 'Oh, that's fabulous! Why would it be bad news?'

'That isn't the bad news, that's the good part. But something's happened, something I wish I could change with the wave of a magic wand.'

Nella's eyes rounded. 'He's had an accident?'

Sofia dropped her gaze to the floor. 'He's been shot. He's pulling through, though. The doctors say he should make a full recovery.'

Nella gasped, bringing her hand to her mouth. 'My goodness, the poor man doesn't deserve that. What happened?'

'That's the thing.' She kept her eyes on the floor, unable to look Nella in the eye. 'I'm the one who caused it all.'

When Sofia dared to glance up she realised Nella's jaw had dropped and the woman with the golden heart was staring silently at her. After a long moment, Nella finally asked, 'How so? Explain it all to me.'

Sofia went over the events of the fateful day, how she'd found herself in the middle of an undercover operation, and it had been too late to get away. 'He saved me. He saved my life by taking the bullet for me, and he's the one paying for my stupidity.'

Nella patted Sofia's hand for a while before she decided to speak. 'I can understand that you feel guilty about all this, Sofia. I know I would if it had happened to me. Still, you shouldn't be too hard on yourself. You saw him in the street with another woman and you had a strong emotional reaction to that. Learn from this mistake, use it to make your life better, and Antonio's too. You can start by apologising to him.'

'I have. And I'm deeply sorry. He knows that and says he forgives me.'

'Good. Trust him, now. Have faith in him. Few men would put your life before theirs.'

'I realise that, too, and I do trust him. I've told him so.'

'Perfect. So now he understands how you feel about him, and you can see that no other man could feel more for you than Antonio. Right? And all this because you walked in on an undercover operation. It wasn't the smartest move, but God knows it has proved useful.'

'I suppose it has.' It warmed Sofia's heart to think that something wonderful, something brilliant, had come of her mistake.

'Don't beat yourself up so much that you miss the silver lining. All right, *cara*?'

Nella's smile filled Sofia's heart with warmth, as did her words. 'Thank you, *zia*. You are one wise woman.'

Nella chuckled. 'I'll accept that. I don't mind a compliment from time to time. Now what are you doing here with your old aunt? Why aren't you at the hospital looking after the man who makes your heart sing?'

'I'll be going there today. That doesn't mean I can't get everything organised for you, and spend some time with you beforehand.'

'Tell me you're not itching to sit next to him?'

That, she couldn't. Sofia pursed her lips. 'It would be a lie.'

'See. Tell me you don't want to drink in his words and maybe even hold his hand?'

'I can't do that, either.' Because as much as she hated hospitals, there was nowhere else she'd rather be. 'But you'll be on your own, *zia*. What if you need something during the day? I could ask Marisa to come back.'

'Sweetie, I feel better than I have in a long time. While Marisa was here yesterday, I went to the bathroom on my own and I even fetched myself a drink and a snack. I can't explain it, but there you have it. I've been praying for a miracle. Maybe this is it.'

'That's wonderful, *zia* Nella. The doctors did say you'd have ups and downs. You're on the up.'

'Definitely on the up. I think that being away from the hospital and doctors and injections is doing me good. And if you're really worried, then yes, we can call Marisa.'

'I'd feel better if she were here with you. I'll get it sorted with her.' She sent Marisa a text, and received an answer almost straight away. 'No problem. She'll be over in half an hour.'

'Great. Thank you. You tell Antonio that I'm thinking of him and I send him my love.'

Sofia's lip twisted with angst. She hadn't told Nella about the security guards in front of Antonio's hospital room, nor that he wasn't the only one who'd be needing them. They were going to have to have strangers in the house too, at least for a while.

Nella frowned. 'What is it? There's something else, I can tell from the look in your eyes. Come on, spit it out. I wasn't born yesterday, remember? These wrinkles on my face should be enough of a reminder. Let them have a purpose, Sofia!'

Sofia giggled. She loved her aunt's way of putting things. It was so colourful. 'Antonio thinks we might be in danger, if the Mafia works out who I am, since he threw himself in front of me to save me.'

Nella brought a hand to her cheek. 'Oh, dear.'

'I called Antonio's colleague, Marta, last night and we had a talk. She doesn't believe there's much risk because she shot the two men who had come to pick up the organs and they are the only ones who saw me.'

'So those two are dead?'

Sofia shook her head. 'I'm not supposed to know, but was told *they're not getting off that lightly.* I imagine they're badly injured and in hospital, or perhaps in custody, in any event out of action for quite a while. That Marta woman is a very good shot, you know. She didn't aim to kill, because *dead scum don't talk,* as she said.'

'Pinch me. I must be dreaming. Or else we're in the middle of some James Bond movie. If it wasn't for poor Antonio being injured, I'd be quite pleased with the turn of events. I never imagined life would become this exciting.'

Sofia smiled. 'From what I understand, they're sending a couple of men over to protect us, even if the risk is minimal at this stage, so I should wait until they arrive.'

Nella's eyebrows shot up. 'Really? They're sending men over here to protect *us*? A bodyguard for you, I can understand, but surely the Mafia isn't going to come after *me*. I've one foot in the grave already.'

Sofia chuckled. 'No, you haven't. I truly believe you can make a full recovery, just like Antonio, and you should believe that too. As long as there's hope, we hold onto it. You taught me that when I was little. I wouldn't be half of what I am if I hadn't had you.'

Nella tilted her head to the side. 'Thank you, *cara*, that's so sweet of you. And let me just say, whether you make mistakes or not, Sofia, I'm very proud of how you turned out.'

Warmth spread through Sofia's body. She hadn't had much encouragement from her parents growing up, and the praise was a soothing balm. 'Thank you.'

Car doors slammed shut at the same time as Sofia's phone chimed with a text. *Our men have arrived at your gate. One 1m75, fair, slim build, the other dark hair, 1m85, medium build. Look through your window. If they don't fit the description, don't open up. Photo coming through. Confirm immediately.*

Sofia looked through the window and at the photo she received on her phone. The men fit the description and if it wasn't them, they were damn good lookalikes. She answered the text. *It's them.*

Good. Check their ID before they enter the house. Armando Ceccone and Pietro Gavone.

Sofia checked their cards and let them in. *ID checked and they're inside. All good. Thanks for your help, Marta.*

No problem. Stay put as much as possible.

I'm going back to the hospital to sit with Antonio.

OK. Don't stop anywhere on the way. You know how to contact me if there are any issues.

Will do. Thanks again, Marta.

Nella smiled at the men in suits who sat with her in the living room. 'Feel free to go whenever you like, Sofia. I'm in good company. Do you gentlemen play *scopa*?'

Sofia chuckled as she imagined her aunt beating them one after the other at the popular Italian card game. 'All right then, I'm off. Call me if you need me to come back, or if you need anything for that matter.'

'I have a feeling I'll be just fine.' Nella's eyes suddenly widened with excitement. 'Oh, I've just realised that when Marisa arrives we'll be four. We can play in teams of two!'

Sofia kissed her aunt goodbye, nodded her thanks to the men that Marta had sent, and hurried back to the one place she really wanted to be, the one place she really felt alive: by Antonio's side.

***

A good night's sleep and especially another heavy dose of painkillers had made Antonio feel so much better that he'd managed, with the help of a nurse, to sit up in bed propped up against a pile of pillows.

He'd been holding his phone in his hand for what seemed like hours, ready one minute to send Sofia a message, the next, only to think it best not to put his words into writing. The less traceable communication, the better. He'd already put her in enough danger as it was.

He finally placed the phone on his lap. She was bound to come and see him at some stage today and then he'd tell her. He closed his eyes. God, it was the worst thing he'd ever had to do, but he'd do it because it meant giving Sofia the best chance to get over it. To get over *him*.

He swore under his breath. Just when he was about to reach paradise with her, it had become hell. It was like missing the lottery by only one number. No, it was much worse than that.

The door swung open and he gulped. *Is it her?*

The security guard was doing a routine check. 'Everything OK?'

Antonio's heart sank, and yet relief rushed through him. He didn't have to face her yet. 'Everything's fine.'

The man in navy blue ducked out as quickly as he'd come in.

Antonio gazed down at his phone again. A message would be so much easier but he'd never gone for easy.

Footsteps, a quiet exchange outside his door, and this time it really was her. Sofia entered, luminous. She'd never been more beautiful, dressed in white, her dark hair bouncing around her shoulders, her smile radiant.

'You're sitting up!' She said it as if he'd performed a miracle. 'You look good.'

And she looked magnificent. If only he could tell her, if only he could cup that beautiful face of hers and kiss those lips, he'd be the happiest man on Earth. But he loved her more than that. He loved her enough to protect her, to save her, to give her a life where she wasn't always looking over her shoulder, wondering if someone was following her. 'I'm feeling a bit better. It must be all the stuff they're pumping into me.'

'You know how you've got the two guards out the front? They've sent men around to the house too. Nella's making good use of them, playing scopa.'

His lips curled up. 'She perhaps shouldn't distract them from their duties.'

'Try telling Nella that. By the way, she sends her love and asked me to tell you she's thinking of you.' Sofia placed her hand on his, her soft, warm hand. 'But not as much as I've been thinking of you.'

'Sofia.' He took a laboured breath. It pained him more than his injury, more than anything, to know that he was going to hurt her. 'Listen, Sofia, there's something I need to discuss with you.'

'Yes?' Her big brown eyes widened with curiosity, and as she leaned closer to him he caught a whiff of her perfume, that mesmerising scent that he could lose himself in without any effort.

The effort, now, was in resisting her. 'I might have said things yesterday ... Well, things I shouldn't have said.'

She stared at him before blinking three times in a row. 'Like what, exactly?'

He looked away. He couldn't bear the shock that had crept onto her face. 'I might have given you the wrong impression.'

She took a sharp breath. 'About what?'

He hesitated. If he said what he had planned, she probably would never forgive him. Then again, that was what he wanted, wasn't it? If she didn't forgive him, she'd stay away from him.

Don't think, Antonio. Just do it, for goodness' sake.

'About us. About where this, this thing between us, is going.' He swallowed to ease the lump that had formed in his throat. 'I've given you the wrong impression.'

'You said that you needed me, and I said I needed you too. Remember?' Her bottom lip quivered. 'How can that result in the wrong impression?'

'I wasn't thinking clearly when we spoke. I'd just woken and realised I was injured. I wasn't sure you were alive. And then, when I realised you were, I was overjoyed. The emotion was so strong it made me say things I shouldn't have. Plus all the medication they'd pumped into my system ... It affects how you think, you know?'

Her whole body shivered briefly. 'I don't understand. You don't feel the way you said you did about me?'

'It's not exactly that. I wasn't thinking clearly about what it would mean, about my situation. Sofia, I have guards in front of my door because my life is at risk. I can't drag you into this. You deserve better.'

'You have no idea how happy I've been since we last spoke. I didn't know someone could be this happy.'

'Sofia, you'd be the first person they'd go after, to punish me.'

'You can protect me, right?'

'I can't even protect myself properly. This isn't the first time it's happened. I was shot last month, too, although the injury was very superficial. I came to Sant'Agosto to go into hiding. Look at how that worked out, and it turns out they weren't even looking for me down here, they were setting up their organ trafficking business.'

'So that's what the doctor meant when he said you couldn't make a habit of it. You'd already taken a bullet. How do you do that, Antonio? How do you carry on like nothing's happened when people have shot you?'

He let out a deep breath. 'I just do. But the best way for me to protect you, Sofia, is to not be in your life.' He closed his eyes for an instant. He had to be strong no matter how much it cost him. He had to be strong *for her.* She deserved better than a life of fear, an early death or becoming a widow.

She let her head fall into her hands. 'This can't be happening. You matter more than any man ever has and I'm so glad to have you in my life...' She gazed into his eyes. 'I love you. There. I've said it. I love you and I know you can feel it too. You love me. If you want me to go away, tell me you don't love me.'

'Sofia, try to understand.'

'Tell me you don't feel it. Tell me you don't feel anything for me and I'll go.'

'That's not the point.'

She tapped his forearm once, twice, three times. 'Yes, it is. That is the point. It's the whole point of life. If we love each other we should share our lives.'

'Stop it, Sofia. Think about it. You won't have a life if you're with me. There's a very good chance it will be cut short—it nearly was—and I can't let that happen.'

'So that's it?' Tears streamed down her cheeks.

He had to look away or he'd give in to his need to feel her against him, to know that she'd be near, to share his days, his nights, everything he ever had, with her. 'I'm really sorry. I made a mistake. I should have known better than to have dinner with you. I should have known better than to drag you into this world I live in. I should have stayed away from the very beginning, the minute I saw you at Nella's. I guess the temptation was too strong. I want you so much, but this last mission has made it quite clear to me that I can't be with you. I hope you'll forgive me one day.'

Her chest heaved as she stood, crying.

It was just as well he was a prisoner of his hospital bed, otherwise he would have wiped her tears, held her against him and kissed her until he'd forgotten all about leaving her. He could already barely remember why he was doing this, and yet he had to hold onto his resolve.

For her. For Sofia. The only woman he'd ever loved.

She walked slowly to the door. Before she pushed it open, she turned to him. 'Why?'

'Why what?'

'If the life you lead stops you from loving people, why do you do it? Do you love your job more than anything?'

He shook his head. He wasn't a mad career person whose ambition prevailed over all else. 'I do it for all the small businesses that are extorted, for the wives whose husbands and sons are tortured and killed because they denounced someone in the Mafia. I do it for the kids that are orphaned every day by the Mob, and for entire villages that live in fear. I do it because I'm needed. This country, my country, needs me.'

And in the first place, he'd done it for her, to impress Sofia, to be worthy in her eyes. Look at how that had worked out.

She nodded with all the hurt in the world on her face, and walked out.

When the door stopped swinging, Antonio finally let his head fall back on the pillow, rolled the sheets into his fist and sobbed silently.

Chapter 15

Antonio put his razor on the shelf in the tiny hospital bathroom, and splashed on some cologne. He liked a clean shave, even if it wasn't going to be noticed by anyone he wanted to please. The only person he cared enough about to try to please was Sofia and he'd put an end to that relationship, for her sake.

It had been the right thing to do, although it hurt. He hadn't realised just how much it would pain him, like a hungry caterpillar eating its way through his heart until there was nothing but emptiness in his chest. It hurt that he couldn't see her chocolate eyes anymore. It hurt that he hadn't felt her warmth in a month, or run his fingers through her shiny hair. It hurt that she wasn't going to be there waiting for him now that he was almost ready to be discharged. He'd healed fast, and he would have loved nothing better than for Sofia to applaud his recovery, wrap her arms around him and welcome him back with a tender kiss. More than anything, it hurt that he wouldn't have a future with her in it.

Why had he told her that he couldn't be with her? Wearing only his pyjama pants, the scar on his chest, long and red, was hard to miss. He stared at it in the mirror. That was why he couldn't be with Sofia, and he'd been lucky this time. Again. How long would his luck last? Not forever, he was sure of that. Look at what had happened to judge Giovanni Falcone, all those years ago, blown up in his armoured car on the motorway, with his wife by his side. The people fighting organised crime in Italy had put a serious dent in it since the 1990s, but the risks of retaliation were as real and as serious as ever, especially now that Onorio's brother had been arrested.

'*Buongiorno*. Anybody here?'

The familiar voice came from his hospital room. Antonio left the bathroom to find the head of the ROS unit standing at the foot of his bed. 'Commander Carone! I wasn't expecting a visit.' Certainly not from his boss who hadn't always seen eye-to-eye with him, and on his last day in hospital.

'I hope it's a good surprise.'

Antonio slipped on his pyjama top and buttoned it up. 'Depends on what you've come to say.' It had to be big news for Carone to travel all the way down from Rome. 'There have been developments with the case?'

'Yes. One of the men Marta shot down, Peppe Mazzoni, has talked. We're still working on it, but what we know so far is that there's a new branch setting up shop down here, to concentrate on the hospitals and clinics of the region. Organs, drugs, and forcing doctors to fix up their men without leaving behind any hospital records. Your assistant, hmm...'

'Gina?'

'Whatever her name is. She said you thought one of the men you saw in town looked familiar. Mazzoni tells us some of the guys working around here were sent down from Rome by Onorio himself, and according to him Onorio's golden boy, Tozzi, has been pretty active. And from facial reconstructions we think he was there the day you were shot in Rome, when you went out to get lunch.'

'So that's why they looked familiar! I couldn't remember anyone except Onorio from that first shooting, but it must have been in here somewhere.' He tapped his forehead. The workings of the mind were certainly a mystery. It was a relief in more ways than one to find out that he had been right all along, confirmation that he hadn't been paranoid. 'Guess I'm not going crazy after all.'

'Guess not.'

'That is a good surprise.'

The commander chuckled. 'Yes, but there's more. Big changes lie ahead.'

Antonio turned his palms up to the ceiling. 'What kind of big changes?' He knew from experience that not all changes were welcome, especially when they were announced by his superiors.

'I'm taking a sideways step.'

'Meaning?'

'I'm going to be running for president.' He clicked his tongue. 'Of the country, in case you're wondering.'

Antonio blinked a couple of times. He certainly hadn't seen that coming. 'Are you sure you want to do that? I'd bet my bottom dollar that the job is just as shitty as this one, and nowhere near as stable.'

Carone let out a hearty laugh. 'I'm well aware of it, but it's time for a change. Or a divorce. Mind you, the latter might happen even if I'm elected.'

If anyone knew the impact of this job on relationships, it was Antonio. 'I wish you all the best, Commander. Congratulations. I mean it.' He held out his hand, and Carone, who hadn't always treated Antonio with affection, shook it grinning ear-to-ear.

'Thanks, De Santis. It means a lot to me.' The commander placed his hands on his hips. 'There's something else, and it's the real reason I came down here.'

'Oh?' Antonio frowned. Carone was probably going to tell him they were bringing in some big shot from the Ministry of Defence to replace him.

'Things haven't always been easy between us, but you've worked hard over the years. You've fought the toughest battles and never backed down. You've got what it takes to loosen the Mafia's grip on this country for good. The job's yours, Commander De Santis.'

Antonio's heart swelled with pride. He really had worked hard. He had made sacrifices. He had risked his life. He was thrilled that his turn to be at the helm of this special unit had arrived. And yet almost instantly a voice in his head told him, as clearly as if someone were yelling into his ear, that it wasn't what he needed most. 'I'm honoured, Commander.'

Carone tapped him on the back. 'You start in a month.'

Antonio cleared his throat. 'I'm truly honoured, but I can't accept the position.'

The Commander's eyebrows shot up. 'What the hell are you talking about, De Santis?' His tone was gruff. 'Have you gone mad?'

Antonio shrugged. 'Maybe.' If madness was having the lucidity to finally realise that people made their own hell and it was time to move on from his, then he had lost his bearings completely. He was OK with that.

'This country needs you, De Santis. If everyone backed down when the going got tough, where would we be? We may as well hand over all power to the *Cosa Nostra*.'

Antonio huffed. 'Look who's talking. You're getting out, aren't you?'

'That's altogether different. My wife is threatening to divorce me and you, you have no wife. Besides, who the hell am I going to appoint if not you?'

'I believe in what I do, and as you said, I've worked very hard. I've devoted a decade and a half of my life to this fight and I don't regret it one bit. My wife left me because of it, and I don't blame her. I'm not saying that I won't one day be involved in this fight again, nor that I no longer believe in the cause, because I do, truly, and I always will. But now is a good time for me to pass on the torch. There is someone just as dutiful and hard-working, just as dedicated and deserving of the position who's gone unnoticed for far too long. Someone who knows the ins and outs of this job, who knows everything I do and brainstorms with me relentlessly. It's Norello.'

'Norello, huh?'

'Yes, sir, the assistant, whatever her name is, as you put it. Gina Norello.'

'A *woman?*'

'She's definitely got what it takes. I'm sure of that. More than any man I know.'

Carone lifted an inquiring eyebrow.

'Except you, of course, Commander.'

'A woman, huh.' Carone turned his palms up to the ceiling. 'What do I care, after all. I'm leaving. Are you sure you won't regret this, De Santis?'

Antonio took a deep breath. He'd longed for the position, had dreamed about it over the years, but he knew in every fibre of his being that this was right. Even if it so happened that what he had in mind for the next part of his life didn't work out. 'No, sir, no regrets. I'm sure of that too.'

***

Sofia finished cleaning the floor and turned off the vacuum cleaner to change attachments in order to pick up the few crumbs she could see on the couch, although it hardly needed it. Now that Nella was feeling better she spent more time in the garden, lounging about on her long chair, and sometimes even pottering around. She had showed nothing but improvement over the past month and although they were waiting for more test results, Sofia was beginning to believe that Nella had a lot of life left in her.

As the roar of the vacuum cleaner died down, Nella's giggle filled the air. '*Si, si.* You have no idea how pleased I am. That's excellent news.'

Who was she ringing from under the patio? And what was their exciting news?

A voice replied. An unmistakable voice, one that sent a shiver down Sofia's spine.

Antonio! He was out of hospital? What was he doing here?

Panic strangled her and she brought a hand to her chest. Breathing in deeply, she tried her best to calm down.

He must be going back to Rome. He's come to say goodbye to Nella. That's the only reason why he'd be here.

She stared at the vacuum. Should she put it away? No, there wasn't time. It was better to head to the bathroom and lock herself inside. If he came into the house, she'd pretend she was having a shower or washing her hair. He wouldn't stay long then, and she'd have the perfect excuse not to chat. It would be fine. He probably didn't want to see her, either.

'Sofia!' called Nella from outside.

Sofia's heart beat faster as she turned away and took a few steps towards the bathroom.

'*Ciao*, Sofia.' Damn it! It was too late. Antonio was in the living room, his deep voice stopping her in her tracks.

She turned and glanced at him, and it was enough to fill her stomach with the liveliest butterflies. He was gorgeous in his navy polo and jeans, more casual than he'd been the past few times she'd seen him and somehow more relaxed in his posture too. 'You're already out of hospital?'

He smiled. 'I don't like sticking around those kinds of places too long. You look great.'

Her lips twisted. He looked more than great, he made her go weak at the knees, made her remember that she was all woman. 'Thanks. You too.' She pointed to the bathroom. 'I'll leave you with *zia* Nella. I was about to go in and do my hair.'

Nella poked her head through the doorway. 'Your hair? You did it this morning.'

Antonio glanced at the vacuum cleaner still out, the upholstery attachment left on the couch. He'd probably heard it from outside too. She wasn't fooling anyone by pretending to suddenly have to go doll herself up in the bathroom. She sighed.

He smiled kindly at her, with such warmth in his gaze that she nearly forgot that he'd rejected her the last time they'd met.

Don't pay attention. He doesn't want you in his life.

Easier said than done. How did she stop her heart from beating so loudly that she could barely hear herself think? How did she put an end to the trembling of her hands, to the dizziness she experienced every time their eyes met? And when he spoke, it wasn't her hands but the entire Earth that trembled beneath her. Why couldn't she just forget him and get on with it?

'Would you like to go for a walk, Sofia? There are a few things I need to say to you.'

Should she go? Why couldn't he just tell her here and now that he was going back to Rome, and be done with it? 'I'm in the middle of things here. I haven't even finished vacuuming the couch, as you can see.'

Nella came in, walked over to the sofa and lay on it, sighing with pleasure as she put up her feet. 'What you can do now is put the vacuum cleaner away, and that will take all of two seconds. And then, go for a walk, Sofia. It'll do you good. You haven't seen Nino for a month, and he has some big news.'

Did Nella have any idea of how hard it was for Sofia to be with Antonio De Santis? Did she even know what it was like to want a man so much it hurt, and still for it to make no difference to him? Nino didn't want her, he'd made that patently clear. It was because he didn't want to put her at risk, and that was a noble cause, but the result was the same as if he'd thrown her away for no reason: she was alone and it was a struggle not to think of him when she lay awake in bed at night, unable to sleep.

Sofia shrugged, doing her best to play down her feelings. 'I bet I can figure out your big news. You're going back to Rome, aren't you?'

Antonio shook his head. 'Actually, no, I'm not.'

'Oh? You've been posted somewhere else?' Possibly somewhere even further away, somewhere she'd probably never see him again. It made no difference since he wasn't with her and yet her heart sank.

'That's not it, either.' His lips curled up. 'Why don't we take a stroll and I'll tell you everything?' He leaned against the wall, seeming even taller now that he'd lost a little weight in hospital. If she let herself go, she'd press her body against his, kiss those lips that called out to her. He raised his eyebrows playfully. 'I'll tell you everything you've ever wanted to know and been too scared to ask.'

She smiled cautiously. 'I've never been too scared to ask anything.'

'Well, then, everything you've ever wanted to know and been too lazy to ask.'

She giggled. Damn it, he always reached her. He was too much fun, too attractive, and altogether irresistible. 'I don't know. I have lots to do this morning.' Mundane tasks that could wait and that she'd be quite happy to avoid, but he needn't know that.

'We'll come back whenever you want. All you have to do is say the word.'

She sighed. 'I guess I'm running out of excuses.' The truth was, the more her gaze met his, the less she wanted to find an excuse to avoid him.

'Great. We'll be back in a little while, then, Nella. Is there anything you need before we go?'

'Just some peace and quiet.' Nella waved them off, a twinkle in her eye. 'Don't you worry about me. You young ones go and enjoy yourselves.'

'I have my phone,' said Sofia, grabbing a small handbag with a few essentials. 'Ring me if you need anything.'

She kissed Nella on the cheek and led the way into the garden, aware of Antonio's eyes on her as he followed her into the bright morning.

'Which way shall we go?' he asked at the gate.

'I don't know.' It wasn't important to Sofia. She wasn't sure she'd notice anything on the walk, neither the bushes that were still green alongside the country road despite the hot beginning to the summer, nor the last of the glorious red poppies in the yellow fields. The simple truth was that she only had eyes for Antonio. 'Do you have a preference?'

He shook his head, his expression sincere. 'As long as I'm with you, I don't care about anything else.'

It warmed her heart that he should say so, although the pleasure was tinged with sadness. If he really didn't care about anything else, he'd stay with her.

They decided to go right, towards the old fountain fed by a spring that came straight from the mountains, where Sofia's grandmother had washed her family's clothes all her life by rubbing them against the grey stone. The road to the fountain was narrower than the one Nella lived on, so narrow in fact that two small cars couldn't pass each other without one of them pulling over to the side, a path so intimate that Sofia wanted nothing more than to hold Antonio's hand and rest her head against his shoulder.

'My boss came down from Rome yesterday to see me in hospital.'

'He left the visit a bit late. Still, that's nice of him.'

'I suppose so, except it wasn't just a courtesy visit. He actually offered me a promotion.'

Sofia stopped and turned to him. Unless he was being sent away, the only position above Antonio's was Commander. 'Is Commander Carone leaving?'

'Yes, he is. It hasn't yet been announced, so please keep it confidential.'

Commander. The man who made her heart beat was being made Commander of the ROS Unit. He would be on television often, in the papers, on the radio. He would become one of the best known faces in all of Italy. He would be famous.

And he would be at even greater risk.

She forced a smile. 'So it's going to be Commander De Santis ... I'm happy for you, truly. You deserve the promotion more than anyone.' Her jaw tightened. She knew she would worry about him, even if they weren't together, but now was not the time to say so. She started walking again so she didn't have to look him in the eye. Hopefully he wouldn't realise that it wasn't joy she felt. It was more akin to dread.

'Thank you. I have to say you don't look that happy about it.' He bent his neck, coming closer to her face, but she did her best to ignore him, keeping her eyes on the road.

After an instant he grabbed her arm and stopped her. 'Sofia, look at me.'

She couldn't, not without spoiling his joy.

'Hey. Come on.' With his thumb on her chin, he gently turned her face towards his. 'I didn't accept the position.'

Her eyes widened as they met his. 'What? But *why?*' Her mind raced. Had he been offered another position elsewhere? Was he going overseas? Did he have to get away, and if so, why? Was he in even greater danger than before and going into hiding, changing his identity to escape the Mafia? Had she done this to him by interfering in his mission? God, she hoped not.

He cupped her face in his hands. She should have pulled away from this man she couldn't be with, should have run from him as fast as she could, except that her whole body melted along with her resolve. Her legs turned to jelly and she needed support, something to hang onto so as not to collapse. She placed her hand on his forearm and that was all it took for him to pull her to him and wrap his arms around her.

'Please, Antonio, don't play with me. This past month has been so very hard. It was such a big step for me to trust someone again, and then you told me that we couldn't be together. It broke my heart.'

'I'm sorry. I've been such a fool. The past month has been excruciating for me too. When Carone offered me the position, I was flattered. It was what I'd been hoping for, for years. And yet I knew immediately that it wasn't what I needed nor even what I wanted.'

He placed his index finger under her chin and lifted it ever so slightly to gaze even deeper into her eyes. 'I need you, Sofia, nothing but you. Please forgive me for the hurt I caused you. I was trying to protect you, rather awkwardly, I admit it, but that's what I was hoping to do. Protect you, because you're the most precious thing in the world. I've resigned.'

'You've resigned from your job? What are you going to do?'

'I'm not sure. I'll figure something out. What I do know is that if I'm no longer in the ROS, no longer fighting organised crime, the attention will be directed away from me. There will be much less risk. Over time, I'll be forgotten. I can change my name, too, go and live somewhere else, Australia if that's what you want. Maybe Nella can come with us. I'll do whatever it takes to keep you safe and to make you feel safe, as long as you come with me. I promise I'll be careful not to burn dinner and I won't scream if it happens. And if you freak out at times because of what's happened in your past, we'll do whatever it takes to work through it. I want you in my life, Sofia. Will you have me?'

She blinked back the tears that threatened to roll down her cheeks. She'd expected everything except this, and life had far surpassed her expectations. She pressed her hand against his.

Worry furrowed his brow. 'What do you say, Sofia?'

Drowning in his grey-green gaze, she answered him, her voice cracking. 'I was ready to take my chances when you were a prime target for the Mafia. I say yes, Antonio. Wherever you want to live, whatever you want to do, I say yes to you, to everything you want, to everything you are.'

He drew her to him, pressing his firm body against hers, and kissed her. His passion burned through her and she hung onto him while his lips asked for more, tasting every bit of hers, exploring her face, her neck, her shoulders.

'Sofia, I've never wanted anyone this much,' he whispered, panting.

'Come.' She took his hand and led him down to the stream, to the place where bushes grew thick and green.

'We can go to my house, if you'd rather,' he said as they stopped.

She shook her head, unable to wait one moment longer. She slipped off her dress, placing it on the grass, and they lay on top of it. He ran his hands up and down her body, kissed her breasts feverishly. Fire burned through her belly as he worked his way down her. When she couldn't resist any more, she placed her hands on his buttocks and pulled him to her, and he entered her, filling her with pleasure. They made love to the sounds of the bubbling water, and the breeze in the leaves of the trees, first in gentle, tender rhythm, and then with passion, with fury and the insatiable hunger of those who have spent years waiting for each other. Sofia cried out in exquisite pleasure, digging her nails into his flesh, and he thrust into her until he could no more, moaning as he came. And then she straddled him and they started all over again.

'I love you, Sofia,' said Antonio as he kissed each of her eyelids before collapsing next to her when they'd finished.

She laughed. 'I love you too.'

He grabbed a blade of grass and tied it in a circle. 'You are the one woman in the world I've always wanted and needed. I knew we were meant for each other from the minute I laid eyes on you, I just didn't know how to tell you back then that you were perfection. You *are* perfection. Please marry me, Sofia. It's not much of a ring, but I'll buy you one tomorrow.'

She let out a scream, the emotion so intense that she could neither speak nor move. His hand rubbed her arm slowly and after a moment she leaned into him, putting all her weight, all her love, all her heart onto him. 'Yes, my darling, I'll marry you. And I'll treasure this ring forever.' She slipped it on and they held each other for the longest time, skin against skin, hope against hope, dream against dream.

When they heard the sound of chatter and barking dogs nearby, they jumped to their feet, dressing as fast as they could, and they ran off laughing like excited teenagers who'd made love for the very first time.

***

A car was parked in front of Nella's house when they got back. As they approached, Sofia recognised the white Alfa Romeo. Her heart raced. 'That's the doctor's car. I hope everything's all right.' Antonio squeezed her hand.

They hurried through the garden to the front door. 'Zia?'

'In here, *cara mia*.' Nella was sitting at the dining table with a stunned look on her face, sharing a glass of almond liqueur with Doctor

Linoni. Sofia couldn't remember the last time she'd seen her aunt drink any alcohol. Either the news was very bad or very good. Sofia froze, too scared to ask.

'Is everything OK?' Antonio looked from Nella to the doctor, bravely seeking the truth as if he'd sensed that Sofia wasn't sure she could face it.

'You're not going to believe this,' gasped Nella, gesturing for the doctor to go ahead.

'Nella is in remission,' said Linoni, grinning. 'She's well. She can do anything, go anywhere, catch a plane back to Australia with you, Sofia, if she wants. We'll check on things next year, but in the meantime, enjoy life, Nella.'

In remission? *Remission!* Just when she thought the day couldn't improve, joy rushed through Sofia's veins from her head to her toes, pure, unadulterated glee that was impossible to contain. She screamed like a child who'd seen the real Santa Claus and jumped into Antonio's arms.

As he spun her around, she laughed until her whole body ached, and she cried without restraint. 'Everything's fine,' she said still chuckling when he finally put her down.

He nodded, his eyes shining with true happiness. 'Everything's perfect, my darling, and it's only going to get better.'

She couldn't imagine what could be better than this day, but if he said so, Sofia believed him. She trusted him with her life, her heart and her soul, and if there was one thing she knew without a shadow of a doubt, it was that as long as they were together, their world would be as beautiful as the most glorious Italian summer.

Thanks for reading *A Shot at Amore*. I hope you enjoyed it.

If you liked this book, here is my other title *His Christmas Feast.*

Sign up to our newsletter romance.com.au/newsletter/ and find out about new releases, must-read series and ebook deals at romance.com.au.

Reviews can help readers find books, and I am grateful for all honest reviews. Thank you for taking the time to let others know what you've read, and what you thought.

Share your reading experience on:

Facebook

Instagram

romance.com.au

Bestselling Titles by Escape Publishing...

Discover another great read from Escape Publishing...

His Christmas Feast
Nora James

One gourmet party. Six potential couples. The taste of love?

After his girlfriend runs off with another man, French chef Christophe Duval swears to stay away from women. That all changes when his sexy neighbour Emily Brighton turns up at the lavish Christmas party he throws at his country home in Marandowie. The trouble is, Emily is the queen of mixed signals and Christophe is along for a rollercoaster ride like no other. Will he ever understand her? Will he ever tame her? Or will the fence they set out to build between their two properties keep them apart for good?

www.ingramcontent.com/pod-product-compliance
Lightning Source LLC
Chambersburg PA
CBHW011556010726
47495CB00010B/2805